"I've never gone home with someone I just met before."

Evan smiled. "I'm flattered."

She didn't smile back at him; she was dead serious.

"I know that about you, Selena," he added. "I could tell. Besides, you mentioned it about forty times that night."

Now her lips did curve upward slightly. "So I did. Sorry about that."

"No need to apologize. The night was... a good one. Very good. But you mustn't think so, the way you're acting."

"It...wasn't a bad night at all." Frowning, she stumbled over what to say next.

"Tell me what's bothering you." The tenderness in his words, his actions, struck her hard, and she sat there in silence, fighting back sudden, embarrassing tears.

He didn't have any inkling how his life was going to change. She wished she could prepare him somehow. Really, she did. Ease him into the truth.

She took a deep, shaky breath and closed her eyes. "I'm pregnant."

Dear Reader,

Fear seems to be a recurring theme in the books
I've written so far: fear of loss, risk, commitment,
change, love. In *A Little Consequence,* Selena Jarboe's
life is ruled by the fear of losing those she loves—
with good reason. She's experienced heartbreaking
loss in the past.

In an effort to run away from her fear, she lands in
the arms of Evan Drake, firefighter, charmer, ladies'
man. A man who places himself in danger every time
he goes on duty. And that's a risk Selena can't live
with. Or so she thinks.

But sometimes consequences have a way of
steering life in a totally different direction from
what we expect....

I hope you enjoy reading Selena and Evan's road
to overcoming what scares them most and
watching them end up with what they need more
than anything.

For more information on this book or others in
THE TEXAS FIREFIGHTERS series, please visit my
Web site at www.amyknupp.com, or feel free to
contact me at amyknupp@amyknupp.com.

Thanks for picking up *A Little Consequence!*

Amy Knupp

A Little Consequence
Amy Knupp

TORONTO • NEW YORK • LONDON
AMSTERDAM • PARIS • SYDNEY • HAMBURG
STOCKHOLM • ATHENS • TOKYO • MILAN • MADRID
PRAGUE • WARSAW • BUDAPEST • AUCKLAND

Recycling programs
for this product may
not exist in your area.

ISBN-13: 978-0-373-71652-4

A LITTLE CONSEQUENCE

Copyright © 2010 by Amy Knupp.

ABOUT THE AUTHOR

Amy Knupp lives in Wisconsin with her husband, two little consequences, er, *sons,* and five (feline) beasts. She graduated from the University of Kansas with degrees in French and journalism and feels lucky to use very little of either one in her writing career. In her spare time, she enjoys reading, college basketball, addictive computer games and watching big red fire trucks race by. To learn more about Amy and her stories, visit www.amyknupp.com.

Books by Amy Knupp

HARLEQUIN SUPERROMANCE

1342—UNEXPECTED COMPLICATION
1402—THE BOY NEXT DOOR
1463—DOCTOR IN HER HOUSE
1537—THE SECRET SHE KEPT
1646—PLAYING WITH FIRE*

*The Texas Firefighters

A thank-you again goes out to the retired firefighter who provided so much information for this and the other books in the series. He deserves a medal for his patience with my many questions and what-ifs.

Thank you to Rachelle Grace, for last-minute bar/pick-up line brainstorming help… and for generally being one of the best friends a girl could have.

Thank you, as always, to my family… Justin, Camden, Colton, Mom and Dad, for your patience, support and love.

And finally, thank you to Victoria, who has a knack for digging through the pages I turn in and pulling out the best…and then making me rewrite the rest. She strives to pull the best story possible out of me every single time, and for that, I'm grateful.

CHAPTER ONE

SELENA JARBOE HAD BEEN on some kind of a mission all day.

She'd been on a mission when she'd stormed through the beach house, scrubbing and cleaning everything in sight, getting rid of inch-thick dust, cobwebs and dirt.

She'd been on a mission afterward when she'd showered, slipped on her flirty black-and-silver baby-doll dress, her cropped cardigan and her killer four-inch heels. Likewise when she'd given her hair the right amount of long, loose curls to drape down her back and over her shoulders just so.

Despite all the preparations, she hadn't known what, exactly, her mission was until she saw *him*.

It was laughingly cliché, but their eyes met across the room, and, yes, it was crowded. He stood in a group near the far wall, which wasn't far at all considering the cozy smallness of the bar. He was several inches taller than the people he was with. Dark haired, eyes that glimmered with humor. And a penetrating glance that said he not only saw her but *noticed* her in detail. He was the kind of man who made everything seem all better.

If ever there was a time Selena needed everything to be all better, it was now. Tonight.

She moved farther into the little beach shack bar—the

Shell Shack, the sign said in an uneven but appropriate font—working her way to an empty stool at the end of the main counter. She felt his eyes on her and when she sat down, she looked again. Just for a moment, long enough to smile and feel the kick start of her blood when she found he was, indeed, smiling at her again, too.

Selena shivered and turned her attention to the bartender, who'd just asked what he could get her.

"Sandblasters are two bucks tonight. Keep the cup as a souvenir," the heavyset man with more hair on his chin than his head said.

Selena shrugged. "Might as well."

She started to wonder at her choice as she watched him mix it, counted eight different types of alcohol being poured into the oversize plastic cup with the cartoon turtle on it. Then she thought about her infuriating mother back in Boston. Her stubborn brother on his way to Afghanistan or who knew where.

"Bring it on," she muttered when the guy set it in front of her and took her cash.

Selena took a swig and tried not to grimace. Normally she stuck to wine when she and her friends went out in Boston, but this wasn't the East Coast and it wasn't a wine night. Wine wasn't part of her mission.

Eight kinds of liquor was a good start to what she was shooting for.

Her eyes automatically checked for the tall, sexy, dark-haired man again, and her shoulders dropped when she realized he was gone.

She swiveled partway around on her stool as she sipped from her straw, acting as if she was searching for someone she knew. She was searching, all right, but she didn't know him. Yet.

The interior of the little bar was packed, and between all the people and the two torch-style heaters, the air inside was warm and humid in spite of the open doorways. Thick, clear plastic kept the chilly October Texas night out. An outdoor patio stretched to Selena's left, but there were only a few groups of brave revelers sprinkled at some of the tables.

She scanned the inside crowd again, waiting for someone to take her breath away as her sexy stranger had. There were plenty of men here, lots of good-looking ones, but so far, no one else sent her pulse racing. If she was going to do something stupidly brazen, might as well save it for someone who took her breath away.

As she turned back toward the counter, a man old enough to be her late father and wide enough to be *three* of her fathers leered at her, shooting her a hungry, gold-toothed smile. Selena shuddered.

What in the world was she doing?

She wasn't the kind of girl to go to a bar alone, ever. If she wasn't out for a good time with her girlfriends, she wasn't out, period. And to even think about talking to a man she'd never met just because he had a certain allure and a look in his eye that drew her in? She'd completely lost her mind.

No, she hadn't, actually. Her family had. Every time she thought about them, everything inside her knotted up, coiled like a predatory snake, as if something needed to give, and give soon.

Heat spread across the right side of her body suddenly, and she knew before she looked that *he* was standing there. The man with the sexy smile.

She looked up at him slowly, taking in his thick chest, the cords of muscle along his neck, the hint of moisture on his sensual lips. Finally meeting his cornflower-blue eyes that, yes, definitely held a spark of amusement. Cockiness. *Interest.*

"Hi," she said, so quietly he could probably barely hear her over the crowd.

"Hi." He said it into her ear and she shivered.

Time to say something witty, she thought, searching her mind. If you're going to be reckless, might as well go all out.

She lifted her cup and took a drink. When she set it down, she noticed she'd drunk half of it and was already feeling the effects of the liquor.

"So," she said, flashing him a smile that was a lot more confident than she felt. "Are you the half-full or half-empty kind of guy?"

God, Selena. That was lame.

But the way he looked at her set something inside her on fire and it no longer mattered how dumb she sounded to herself.

"Right now? With you smiling at me? I'm thinking three-quarters full," he said.

"We have something in common, then."

"At least one thing," he said, and passion filled his eyes, the rim of blue shrinking as his pupils expanded. "Not a bad pickup line. Mind if I use it sometime?"

"As long as you don't try to use it on me."

"Would I need to?" His voice went gravelly, somehow more intimate even though they were in a crowd. He leaned his elbow on the bar, bringing him closer to her, near enough that she caught his scent—spice and beer mixed with one-hundred-percent red-blooded male.

This close, she could see every nuance of his skin, sun roughened, still tanned, recently shaved. Her fingers itched to touch his face and she imagined what it would feel like. Sandpapery. Strong. Warm.

"Normally I prefer straightforward to games," she said.

With him, she wasn't sure it mattered. She eased in closer. His eyes didn't leave hers and her heart thundered. Her thoughts changed from *was she really going to do this?* to *how could she get him alone?* So she could touch him. Let him touch her, everywhere, fill all her senses with him. Make her forget everything else.

"Normally?"

Selena laughed. There was nothing normal about this situation and he seemed to understand that. "Generally."

"I can do straightforward." He brushed a lock of hair off her cheek and Selena turned toward the contact. She had to will herself not to press her lips to his palm....

"I've got this really great beach outside," he said. "Would you like to see it? So we can be straightforward?"

A shiver of anticipation went through her and a physical ache pulsed deep inside. She nodded, took a final long swig of courage and stood, happily leaving her souvenir cup behind.

"That was kind of a triple line," she told him as he wrapped her hand in his and gestured for her to go first.

"Do I get triple points?"

She waited until they stepped outside the loud interior. "Normally lines count against a guy."

"There's that word 'normally' again. Do you 'normally' leave with a guy you've been talking to for less than ten minutes?"

"No. Do you?"

"I don't normally leave with a guy ever."

"Good to know."

They went down the concrete steps to the sand and turned south. She paused long enough to slip her heels off.

"So why are you here? With me?" he asked. "Straightforward answer."

Instead of replying, she stopped and faced him. The moon was a slender crescent behind him and the waves filled the night with their incessant roar that seemed to insulate them from the rest of the world. As she peered up into his light blue eyes, she felt an invisible current between them. It made her heart trip over itself and her insides turn to liquid.

Their hands were still entwined. A slow smile spread across his face and he lowered his head. Selena stood on tiptoe, dropped her shoes and, with her other hand on the back of his head, pulled him toward her. Just before they kissed she paused.

"What's your name?" she whispered.

He chuckled, a husky sound in his throat. "Evan."

"Evan," she repeated. "I'm Selena. Nice to meet you."

They both moved into the kiss at the same time, closing the space between them as if names couldn't matter less.

He pulled her body in to his and slid his large hands down her back, the heat of him igniting her like no man ever had. Her response was elemental, almost primitive. She felt his hardness against her abdomen and wanted him all to herself, alone.

As soon as possible.

Evan Drake had never met a woman like Selena before—and he'd met a lot of women in his twenty-nine years. He liked to think he could read them well, especially the signals they sent, either purposely or not, in bars. Selena didn't fit into any of the categories, though, as far as he could guess. She wasn't in the habit of picking up men like this, of that he was sure. When she'd first spoken to him, her nerves had shown through, as if she'd had to urge herself to speak at all.

She came across as witty and intelligent, not at all desperate or needy. Although right now she was making no secret that she needed him physically, and frankly, he was right there with her.

He was no angel, not unaccustomed to bringing women he didn't know well to his bed, but something about this girl lit him on fire like never before. Maybe it was that he suspected she didn't do this often if at all. That she'd chosen him.

Hell, who gave a rat's left nut about the whys or the hows when you had a woman like Selena in your arms.

"My place is a couple blocks away," he said, their bodies still aligned, still teasing at each other's mouths.

She nodded and kissed him again and, swear to God, if he didn't get her home in the next thirty seconds they were going to make a spectacle of themselves.

"Let's go." His voice was rough, as if he'd swallowed a mouthful of sand. He took her hand and pulled her gently in the direction of his apartment.

CHAPTER TWO

"FIGURED YOU'D still be in bed," Clay Marlow said when Evan emerged from his bedroom the next morning. "Sleeping for a change." The amusement on his roommate's face told Evan he and Selena had made too much noise. All night.

"What time did you come home?" Evan asked, rubbing his eyes.

"I saw you leave the Shack with her. I stayed till the bar closed. Then I went for a run about four in the morning. Spied her sneaking across the parking lot just after five."

"Sorry, man. Didn't mean for our…uh…didn't mean to drive you away from the apartment."

Clay laughed good-naturedly. "Like hell. Why aren't you asleep now?"

"Going to look at a boat." Evan went into the kitchen and rummaged around for something to eat. He wasn't a breakfast guy, but he'd burned off some serious energy over the course of the night and was ravenous.

"By yourself?" Clay asked, pouring coffee from the coffeemaker into a mug and sticking it into the microwave.

"With Chief Peligni. Going up to Corpus." Evan opened every cupboard, looking for anything edible. "We need to buy some food."

Clay took his mug out, swallowed a gulp and frowned. "Coffee, too. This is yesterday's. What kind of boat did you find?"

"Marine Trader…eighty-seven. One owner, guy who's babied it. I gather it's killing him to sell it but his health is failing and his wife is forcing the issue."

"Sounds promising. You thinking seriously about buying it?"

"If it's as good as it seems, I'll have it out on the Gulf before the end of the year."

"Finally got the money?"

"If I can get him down about ten grand, I have enough for the down payment." He'd been saving for years for his own trawler yacht and the reward was so close he could taste it. He found a half-smashed granola bar on top of the fridge and opened the wrapper.

"Hope it works out," Clay said. "So the girl from last night…"

"Yeah?" Evan's mind wandered to Selena's smooth, milky skin, her soft, perfect curves, the way her glossy hair had draped over his chest. They hadn't slept at all, and yet, he wanted her still. Doubted he could ever get enough of her…

"You going to see her again?"

Evan bit off the uncrushed end of his granola bar and chewed, eyeing Clay. "Why? You got a thing for her?"

"Don't need your rejects, thanks."

"Who said I rejected her?"

"You're sure testy today."

"Didn't sleep much."

Clay chuckled again. "Trust me, I know." He studied

Evan between swigs of leftover coffee. "Did you get her number or what? Why are you holding out?"

"I'm not holding out, man." Evan leaned his head back and dumped the remaining crumbs—half the bar—from the wrapper into his mouth, wishing like hell Clay would lose this nosy interest in his sex life. He took a few steps toward the living room and back. "I tried more than once. Believe me, I'd very much like to see her again." He crumpled the wrapper into a tight ball and met Clay's stare head-on. "She refused to give me her number."

He threw the wrapper on the counter and strode out of the apartment.

It was after two in the afternoon when Selena dragged her tired, sore body out of bed. Sore but sated, she thought with a wicked grin.

She'd gone out of her ever-loving mind last night. Had become a different person. One that had a heck of a lot more fun than her.

Her smile faded as thoughts of her family flooded her. Unfortunately, her reckless night hadn't done anything to dull the pain, the fear.

She took a quick shower then headed to the kitchen for food. Or drink, rather, since she hadn't bought groceries yet. Settling for a can of root beer, she went to the unlit fireplace in the living area and sat on the hearth.

When her dad had had this place built, he'd been told he wouldn't need a fireplace. This was the beach. Southern Texas. But her father had loved a crackling fire and stubbornly insisted on it. He'd had to convince her mother, too. She'd argued for a gas log, because wood-burning fireplaces were more work. Her dad had prevailed, though, since this house was his domain. Her mother had gotten her way on the Nantucket property.

Selena traced her finger along the rectangular perimeter of the fireplace, then pulled back the wire mesh curtain. The inner concrete walls were charred from use. She leaned against the wall next to it and closed her eyes, feeling so close to her dad right now it made her chest tight.

When she was about ten, her family had flown down after Christmas, before school started up again. Every evening, the four of them—her dad, brother, mother and herself—would stay up much later than she was usually allowed, sitting on the floor in front of the fireplace, playing dominoes. Their version was no sedate, polite game—it was high stakes for bragging rights, always a boisterous affair. Those were some of the happiest memories of her childhood, back before her dad died and the family bonds had died with him.

Selena stood and wandered to the tall pine entertainment center. She pulled out the wide drawer, wiggling it just so to get it unstuck. Tears unexpectedly filled her eyes when she saw it—the hand-stitched cloth bag of dominoes.

She carried it back to the hearth, sat on the ceramic tile floor in front of it and dumped the dominoes out with a clatter. One by one, she stood the ivory pieces on end in a wavy line almost without thought, and again, she was carried back to years when her dad was still living.

It was a different trip, that time in the summer, a rainy afternoon. Her mom had been sitting quietly on the sofa watching the three of them with the dominoes, content to be there with her family even though she wasn't part of the action. Selena often wondered if that content woman still existed somewhere inside her mom. She hadn't seen signs of it since her dad was killed on an FBI assignment.

They hadn't been back to this house since. It had been his favorite place and his presence, his personality, was discernible in every single room. This was the only place where her memories hadn't been soiled by the Cambridge-Jarboe discord since they'd become three instead of four—unlike the main house and the Nantucket house they visited each summer.

When the domino train had crashed, she picked up the pieces, stacking several at a time, and dropped them into the bag.

Enough moping. She needed food, and a little shopping pick-me-up. Anything to get her mind off the family she'd walked away from.

ACCESS DENIED.

The automated teller machine seemed to scream at Selena. She glanced behind her to see if anyone was close enough to notice she was having difficulties.

Again she punched in the personal identification number she'd been using for the past, oh, twelve years or so to access her allotted part of the bottomless Cambridge-Jarboe bank account.

Trying the number a third time didn't make a difference. Rejection was rejection.

Her mother had cut her off.

"Dammit." She punctuated the curse by hitting the machine.

"Thanks Mom," she muttered, smacking the button

to cancel the transaction when what she really wanted to do was pound a hole through the ATM with her fist.

She had exactly $423.07 left of the cash she'd taken with her when she'd fled Boston. Had she known this would happen, she would've been a lot more careful with her money. Now, unfamiliar panic pumped through her. What did she know about stretching her dollars?

She rubbed her upper arms and shivered, then gritted her teeth.

Okay, then.

She'd been the one to walk away from her family. Had promised herself she'd be all right on her own. And she would.

Somehow.

Her mother might be laughing at her now from the Cambridge-Jarboe estate, but Selena wasn't about to go crawling back.

She should've guessed her mother would cut her off. Clara Cambridge-Jarboe—don't you *dare* forget the Cambridge—had become the type to use money to her advantage. Selena supposed she herself had been a perpetual victim without really thinking about it, since she lived off her mother's money. The monthly paycheck had never been a bone of contention between them. Rather, Selena suspected it made her mother feel important and needed and, yes, superior, to have her daughter dependent on her. In her mother's mind, it was monthly confirmation that she was right—art was an impractical, useless pursuit for a career.

The ridiculous thing was that Clara had never earned a penny of the family money herself. Her family's wealth dated back several generations, and the only thing she had done to increase their fortune was to hire one of the best money guys to take care of her precious portfolio.

Selena needed money. She'd have to get a paying job for the first time in her life.

She was so far out of her realm of experience she wasn't sure where to start. She turned and walked blindly across the street, toward Lambert's Ice Cream Shoppe. As she approached the door, she spotted a metal newspaper box.

She dug in the bottom of her Gucci for some quarters. Now if only she had some employment experience beyond volunteering and some marketable job skills besides artistic talent she might have some hope.

CHAPTER THREE

Two and a half weeks later

WAS IT the fifteenth? Selena's eyes popped open at this, her first coherent thought of the day.

She sat up straight, cold fear in the pit of her stomach.

October fifteenth.

Two days after her period was due. She was never late, could set a military clock by it. It should've been here when she woke up the morning of the thirteenth— she remembered calculating that last month and rolling her eyes at the unlucky date. Two days ago.

She'd been sidetracked by her job. She'd started it on Monday, thought she was going to puke for most of the day from nerves, but maybe it wasn't nerves after all.

Nauseous now, and light-headed, Selena lay back down, curling on her side, and pulled the blankets over her face. She closed her eyes.

Sleep didn't come. Neither did oblivion, denial or a happier reality. She had to get out of bed and find out for sure.

Her mind strayed to images of babies. Her holding a baby. *Her* baby. Abruptly, she shook her head, unable to handle the mere idea of parenthood. It was too much to think about.

She moved on autopilot through a shower, dressed in skinny jeans and a flowy green and blue shirt. Definitely not clothes that were appropriate for her job painting murals for the city of San Amaro's upcoming twenty-fifth birthday celebration. Lucky for her, she set her own hours. As long as she finished each mural on schedule, she'd continue to get paid.

No way she could work today, unless her suspicions happened to be wrong. She headed off to the corner drugstore to find out.

TWENTY-FOUR MINUTES was all it took for a girl's entire life to change. Four minutes each way to the store in her Saturn SUV, six minutes trying to figure out which brand of pregnancy test to buy, five minutes waiting in line. Reading the directions, unwrapping the package, doing the test.

Waiting.

Turned out that two minutes was an e-freaking-ternity when you weren't breathing, waiting to see if a second line appeared.

It did.

Selena stared at it. Checked the picture on the directions again and, yep, direct match for "congratulations."

She picked up the stick and tried to break it in half. When that didn't work, she hit it on the edge of the counter. Stupid thing was hardy, and for $13.99 she supposed it should be.

She glanced around the master bathroom for a weapon, but there wasn't much, only her cosmetics and toiletries. The wooden-heeled shoes she wore, though…

Determined, she flung the stick to the ceramic floor and stomped on it with her heel, as if it were a venomous spider (never mind that she would run from a spider, not hang around and kill it). The plastic casing finally cracked in several places, but the satisfaction was minimal.

She was still pregnant.

Options flipped through her mind like an old-fashioned Rolodex. Ways out. Like a preachy after-school teen special. All the possibilities sucked.

Leaving the test crushed on the floor, she made a beeline for the stairway. She ascended both flights until she was in the turret room where she'd set up her art supplies. All four walls were windowed, showing the Gulf, the shore, the weather like a nonstop movie reel. There was a door on the water side that opened to a widow's walk. Selena went there now.

Wind whipped her hair, tangling it in seconds. It was colder up here than at ground level. There was a wildness most days as the wind gusted in off the water. She raised her chin and faced it, eyes closed. Out here, constant buffeting by the weather made coherent thought nearly impossible.

Right now, that was exactly what Selena needed.

She held on to the rickety railing, one knee on the weather-beaten wooden bench that wound all the way around, gazing out at where the Gulf gave birth to the waves. They seemingly formed from nothing, gathered momentum and size until they were awe inspiring, intimidating…and then they rolled into nothing once again when they hit the sand.

Selena didn't know how long she stood there watching each wave like a minidrama. Suddenly, exhaustion hit her at the same time reality did. Every muscle in her body felt as if she'd been swimming against a strong current. She backed away from the edge, felt for the door handle behind her and let herself inside. She crossed the floor the few steps to the her dad's chair and collapsed into it sideways.

She would have the baby.

The certainty hit her the second she opened her mind to the possibility. There was only one option that would ever work for her.

When she was a little girl, all of her favorite pastimes had had a domestic, happy-family flavor to them—taking care of baby dolls, playing "house," having tea parties, serving family "dinners" on miniature plastic dishes. Back then, she'd wanted to be like her mother—a society lady, a socialite, a woman head over heels for her husband.

Everything had changed when her dad died. Her mother, especially. As a teenager, Selena had vowed that she would never be the woman her mom had become—detached and distant from her family.

As an adult, she harbored hopes of one day fostering the kind of warmth the Cambridge-Jarboes had known so long ago with her father. She hadn't planned on having the opportunity so soon—now—but she wouldn't squander it.

The biggest question, then, was whether it would be a traditional family of three or a single mother and child. Selena didn't know the first thing about Evan—including his last name—to have an inkling which way it would go.

She methodically, absently, ran her fingers through the tangles in her hair as she wondered about the man she'd made this baby with. What would he do? How would he react?

She wasn't ready to face him yet, but would have to do it soon. She'd left her family and come down here to take charge of her life, forge ahead on her own. Now, ironically, a large chunk of her future depended on one man.

HOURS LATER, after she awoke in her dad's worn chair, Selena left the beach house to walk along the sand. A light drizzle had started, clouds hanging low over the Gulf, the sky and water a study in grays. The silence and emptiness of the beach house had driven her out in search of living, breathing beings, but the shore, too, was deserted. She carried on, without a destination in mind.

After a while, she stood in front of the little grass-roofed bar where her current trouble had started. The Shell Shack.

Heavy-duty plastic again protected the inside from the wind and drizzle. A warm light glowed from within, beckoning Selena to the inner sanctum. As she stepped into its shelter, she breathed in the familiar odor of beer, food and humidity.

The shack seemed larger than it had before, when so many people had been crammed into it. Mostly empty stools lined the semicircular main bar and another curved counter wound around the outer perimeter, facing the shore.

A cute, petite brunette about her age, late twenties or so, smiled at her from behind the bar. Selena walked to the stool on the far left side at the main bar.

"Hi," the bartender said. "What can I get for you?"

Her brown hair was pulled back in a neat ponytail and her green eyes radiated happiness.

"Just…ice water, please." A stack of Sandblaster cups towered on the back counter, a vivid reminder of her last visit here. "I'd like to order some food, too, please."

"You got it." The bartender handed her a tall, skinny menu then set a plastic cup of water in front of her. "My name's Macey. Just holler when you're ready."

"Thank you." Selena glanced over the short list and quickly settled on seviche and nachos. She caught Macey's eye and placed her order, then sat back to watch the people around her. She'd hoped to escape the solitude of the beach house, but watching others in couples and small groups just made her loneliness more pronounced.

"You look kind of down," Macey said as she cleaned the counter in front of Selena. "Everything okay? Sure you don't need something stronger?" Surprisingly, her questions didn't come across as too invasive. Maybe Selena was just *that* happy to be out of the empty house.

She studied this woman for several seconds and leaned closer, the need to unburden herself suddenly overwhelming. "I just found out I'm…pregnant." There. She said it out loud for the first time. Her pulse sped up, her face grew warm, and she couldn't seem to get enough air.

Thankfully Macey didn't overreact and draw attention to them. "Wow. That's a whopper," she said. "Ironic that we can't deal with such a big scary thing with a nice shot or two of tequila, isn't it?"

"A cruel joke," Selena said. Shame threatened to choke her up. Selena wasn't the type to do the wrong thing, to sleep around. Her circle of friends back home would be stunned if they knew what she'd done—and what she would now have to go through. She'd somehow sensed Macey was more understanding, less judgmental, but still...facts were facts. She wasn't proud of how she must come across to this new acquaintance.

A young, lanky guy came out of the back room with Selena's food and set it in front of her.

"Thanks, Ramon," Macey said. He smiled a goofy grin and retreated.

"You're the first person I've told," Selena said quietly. "Guess I needed to confess to someone." She tried to laugh it off.

"What about the father?" Macey asked.

Selena shook her head. "We're not...together." Again with the warm cheeks, and she wasn't one who normally blushed.

"Ooh, you must be overwhelmed."

"Terrified."

The sympathy on Macey's face just about did Selena in. It'd been almost four long weeks since she'd left behind the people who had made up her support system—even if they'd given as much grief as support. She hadn't realized how much being by herself, trying to handle everything on her own for the first time, getting a paying job, had been wearing her down. And then the pregnancy news...

Tears popped into Selena's eyes and her throat swelled. She was not going to embarrass herself by crying here, in public, just because this woman was so kind. She sucked in a lungful of air and wiped her eyes quickly. "Sorry," she told Macey. "I didn't realize I was on the edge."

"I've heard pregnancy hormones can be a real bear."

"Grizzly, apparently." Selena shoved a tortilla chip into her mouth, hoping to distract herself.

"Do you plan to tell him?" Macey asked.

"Soon. I'm still trying to absorb the truth myself."

"Yeah. That might take a few days. Excuse me for a minute." Macey went to the other side of the bar to wait on two thirtysomething women and returned after serving them Sandblasters and placing their orders for burgers. "Sorry about that," she said when she returned. "So what's your next move?"

"Does sticking my head in the sand count?"

Macey grinned. "There's enough sand around here, but that's probably not the best choice. You'd get it in your eyes."

Selena choked out a laugh, then sobered almost instantly. "Next I need to find a long-term job. The one I have will only last for a few months."

"Are you new to the island?"

"I've been here almost a month. Just long enough to really shake up my life."

"Hey." Macey made eye contact with her. "You'll get through this and be okay. Even though it doesn't seem like it right now."

"I don't have much choice, do I?" Selena forced a smile.

"What kind of job are you looking for?"

"Well…" Selena wasn't sure what to say. "I'm open. Something with a regular paycheck. No matter what the father decides, I need to be able to support the baby."

"What kind of experience do you have?"

"I'm embarrassed to admit I never had a paying job before I got here."

Macey's eyes widened. "Never?"

"Since finishing college I've done volunteer work for an organization back in Boston called Art to Heart. It incorporates art and creativity into the lives of at-risk kids."

"Sounds like an amazing place," Macey said enthusiastically. "I started my own nonprofit organization a few months ago. I wish I could hire you, but I don't have a budget for a salary or even a wage yet. Which is part of the reason I'm here. That and my fiancé and I own the place." She swung her arm to indicate the bar.

"Fiancé? Congratulations."

"Thanks!"

"What kind of organization do you have?"

"I help women start their own small businesses. Do you have any talents you could turn into a business?"

"Not really. I'm an artist. It's tough to make a living painting."

Macey eyed her thoughtfully. "Don't be so sure. Let me give it some thought."

"Thank you. I appreciate it." She didn't hold out a lot of hope but at least she had time to figure it out. She took a drink and set her glass down, distracted. "I seem to be revealing all my embarrassing skeletons in the first few minutes I've known you." She lowered her voice, watching her straw as she swirled it in her glass. "My mom's family has always been comfortable, and I've been content to accept whatever she wanted to give me. I loved the kids' organization and felt I was making a difference by working there. Living at home allowed me to do that, so why not?"

"Can't say I blame you."

"I loved it. Loved the kids. They had some serious problems but after interacting for a few weeks or sometimes even just days, a lot of them would come out of their shells and express themselves through art."

Selena managed a smile as she remembered. Rollie, the eleven-year-old who created the best manga she'd ever seen. Malinda, the tiny ten-year-old girl who made beautiful paintings. Jerome—her absolute favorite, though she'd never admit that aloud—the six-year-old boy whose fine-motor-skill development was so far behind he hadn't known how to hold crayons and scribble until she'd worked with him for several sessions. He didn't show particular artistic talent but that wasn't what Art to Heart was about.

"Anyway," Selena continued, "my mom and I haven't been close for a long time and we had a major disagreement. I came down here to start over, and I just found out she closed my access to the bank account. I'm not surprised. Just forced to face reality now."

"What kind of artist are you?" Macey asked. It looked as if her mind was spinning, which encouraged Selena.

"Mostly painting and drawing. I can illustrate on the computer but that's never been my strong point."

"If you could make a living painting and drawing, would you want to?"

"Absolutely."

"I'd like to see your work," Macey said, signaling to another customer she'd be right there. "I've got some ideas. We might be able to figure something out."

Selena didn't dare get her hopes up. But as Macey tended to other customers and Selena finished her seafood, she dug a pen out of her purse and wrote the address of the beach house and her cell-phone number on a napkin. Traffic at the bar had increased and she didn't want to keep Macey from her job any longer. Besides, what if her one-night stand returned here, to the scene of the crime? She tucked the napkin under a twenty and went back out into the damp afternoon, not quite as desolate or hopeless as when she'd walked in.

CHAPTER FOUR

"FOR A LOT OF WOMEN I take on," Macey said as she slowly circled Selena's studio two days later, "we have to really work at coming up with a viable product or service for them to make money on. Selena, you've got it all right here. These paintings are fantastic."

Selena released the breath she'd been holding since she'd led Macey up the stairs to the turret studio. "You think I could make enough to get by for a while?"

"I think you could do more than get by. There are several directions we could take. We could incorporate some of your art on different products, like bags, T-shirts, postcards and a hundred others. I know someone who might be able to help us get it started. And I bet you could get some space for your originals in local galleries, maybe a gift shop or two. Some of these Gulf scenes could garner decent cash."

"You really think people would pay for these?"

"Absolutely. You capture the scenery beautifully and infuse each painting with tangible emotion, even though there aren't any people in them. It's amazing, actually."

Selena sat on the edge of the overstuffed chair and leaned forward, elbows on her thighs as she ran her hands over her face.

"Why do you seem to have trouble believing these

are marketable?" Macey asked, dragging her gaze from the large acrylic of the San Amaro Pier.

Selena straightened and shook her head, trying to get rid of the years-old doubts. "My mother is a firm believer that art is not a profitable pursuit. I guess it's been drilled into my mind now."

"Well, time to dig it out."

"Maybe you're right. After all, the city's paying me well enough for the murals and if we can get this going…"

"*When* we get this going," Macey corrected. "Oh, the murals… I read about that project in the paper last week. That's you?"

"That's me. I'm contracted to do five. The fire station, the nature reserve, the gateway to the city, in a park and in front of City Hall. I have until the end of May to finish them."

"Excellent publicity for your new business." Macey sat on the stool where Selena usually worked and took out her phone to make notes. "Start thinking about a name for your company. I've got information and forms you'll need to fill out and we can meet with the merchandising guy I know in the next couple of weeks."

"Wow. Just like that?" Selena asked.

"If you really want to move forward with this."

Selena didn't hesitate. "I do." Making a living by painting would be satisfying—*beyond* satisfying—on so many levels. "I need to. How else am I going to…" She put a hand on her flat abdomen but didn't finish the sentence. It was still so much to wrap her brain around, and talking about a child, a baby… It had a dizzying, nauseating effect on her.

"Feed the child?" Macey asked sympathetically. "I

think you're smart to become self-sufficient, but I also have to ask… Did you tell the father yet?"

Selena groaned. "Still gathering my nerve. It's at the top of my to-do list."

"Any idea how he'll react?"

Selena laughed. "I don't have a clue." She couldn't bring herself to admit to Macey that she didn't even know his last name or what he did for a living. "Guess I'll find out soon enough. I'll go this evening to talk to him."

"Maybe it won't be as bad as you think."

"Maybe." She'd had all kinds of scenarios running through her mind, most of them not good. The truth was she wasn't really sure what she wanted him to do. Ideally, they would get together, fall in love and marry— not because of their big *whoops*—and live happily ever after. She laughed.

"What's so funny?" Macey said, jerking her out of her thoughts.

"Nothing, actually." Selena closed her eyes. "Maybe I could just paint a baby and leave it on his doorstep. Ring the doorbell and run."

Macey chuckled. "He lives here on the island?"

Selena bent forward again, hesitating. "He does. I might as well get it all out in the open. I don't know this guy. I did something I've never done before in my life. I was emotionally on the edge and went out by myself, feeling completely reckless…"

"And you found some sexy guy to make you forget about your troubles for a night?" Macey's tone was understanding.

"That sums it up nicely," Selena said with an embarrassed grin. "I met him at your bar, as a matter of fact."

"Really? Was I working?"

Selena shook her head and described the bartender.

"Kevin," Macey said with a nod. "Glad the Shack set you up for a really good night but sorry it's turned into a life-changing event." She smiled sympathetically.

"And what's worse?" Selena continued. "If I hadn't gotten pregnant, I wouldn't regret a second of it. Am I proud of it? No." She stared off at nothing, seeing instead Evan's body moving over hers, playing hers like a virtuoso with an expert touch. Just remembering made her tighten with longing.

Selena couldn't help but wonder if Evan was a regular at the Shell Shack. Did he go there enough that Macey would recognize him? Did he always leave with a different woman?

"Confession time?" Macey asked. "I did something similar once." A slow grin spread across her lips. "And to add to the—I don't know—fantasy of it all, it was when I was in Asia with the Peace Corps. A local guy. We barely spoke the same language."

"Something every woman should do once in her life. Just…without the pregnancy part." She took a deep, shaky breath. "You know, we should probably eat dinner before it's completely cold."

"Sounds like a plan." Macey stood up from the stool and linked her arm in Selena's. "It's going to be okay. I'll be here for you no matter what your mystery man says."

Selena couldn't answer. Gratitude swelled in her throat and if she spoke she'd end up crying like a baby.

She'd struck it lucky when she'd run into Macey at the bar.

Still, there was only so much Macey could do. This was Selena's mess. Hers and Evan's. Or maybe just hers, depending on what happened later.

She suddenly wondered how she would get any dinner down at all.

MACEY, THE TRAITOR, hurried off as soon as they finished eating, not wanting to enable Selena to procrastinate from her all-important visit any longer.

Conveniently, Selena could stall on her own just as easily. She changed her clothes—twice. Painted her toenails in a dark shade called eggplant. Touched up her eyeliner and added lip gloss. Considered pulling one of the ancient tomes off the shelf in the living room and reading it in its entirety before setting out to see Evan.

"The sooner you go, the sooner you can get it over with," she said out loud, frustrated with her own cowardice.

It was nearing seven. If she waited much longer, he could, God forbid, be out on a date or something equally humiliating. Calling him first would've been easier, but she'd been emphatic about not exchanging phone numbers. Her only option was to just whisk in and deliver her news.

She went into the master bathroom and checked her appearance in the full-length mirror on the back of the door one last time. Holding her hand to her abdomen, she straightened, looking for any sign of a baby bump. Her pants were tighter than usual but that was probably more from dinner than a microscopic fetus.

Morning sickness hadn't been major yet and had

stayed true to its name, rolling through her only when she woke up each morning. Soda crackers had become a permanent fixture on her nightstand and eating two or three before she got up seemed to make the nausea subside.

Right now, however, she regretted the Chinese take-out she and Macey had plowed through. She went to the kitchen in search of more crackers. They hadn't failed her yet.

Half a package later, Selena washed down the last of the crumbs with a glass of water. She brushed her teeth a second time.

"No more putting it off. Let's go, self."

Grabbing her purse, more for security than an actual need for anything in it, she headed out the door to her SUV.

She'd never admit it to anyone, but she'd driven by Evan's apartment a few times since their private slumber party, before finding out she was pregnant. The first time had been a test to see if she could find it again after leaving so fast the morning after and walking home. After that, it'd just become a habit of sorts. She had no idea why she did it—it served no purpose. There were no windows on the street side of his apartment, so she couldn't catch a glimpse of him. She didn't even know what kind of vehicle he drove so she couldn't keep tabs on whether he was home or not. She hadn't had any illusions about seeing him again, so she wasn't sure what was up with her stalker act.

Tonight she drove down the street and then instead of turning into the small lot for his apartment, she kept going.

"Chicken. Just do it. What's the worst that could happen?"

Let's see… He could slam the door in her face. He could yell and scream and rant. He could call her names or blame the pregnancy on her.

After turning around in a residential driveway down the street, she came back and pulled in. There were several cars in the lot, so hopefully he was here.

Her heels on the sidewalk seemed extraordinarily loud, as if announcing to the entire complex that she came bearing important, life-altering news. She climbed the stairs on tiptoe in an attempt to keep it quiet.

Second floor. Last door on the right. Her skin heated as she remembered the night with Evan. They'd managed to keep their lust mostly under wraps until they got into his apartment and shut the door. Then he'd nearly leaped for her after he locked the door, but he hadn't had to leap far because she'd been practically attacking him.

Then she'd become crazed with a desire that no other man had ever awakened in her.

Selena stared at the door. Trying to summon the courage to knock.

A car pulled up in the parking lot, compelling her to act so she wouldn't be caught standing here like an idiot.

Here goes nothing.

She knocked firmly on the solid door, thankful there was no peephole.

Footsteps approached from the other side of the door and it swung open. Evan's roommate stared down at her for a couple of seconds before speaking. "We meet again."

She tried to smile but wanted to melt into the floor. She'd run into this guy in the parking lot after leaving Evan, hair messy, clothes not quite right. "Is Evan here?"

"Evan!" he hollered. "Someone's here to see you! Come on in." He stood back. "I'm Clay."

"Hi." Selena cautiously glanced around. Oh, yeah, she remembered this place in detail. How could she not? They'd...well, they'd certainly not made it to the bedroom for round one that night.

"Selena," Evan said as he entered the living room, eyebrows raised in surprise. "What are you doing here?"

"Nice," his roommate said sarcastically.

"It's good to see you." Evan moved closer and she tried to fight her physical reaction to him. It was a losing battle as he practically loomed over her with his wide, muscular shoulders and chest and those clear blue eyes giving her all of his attention.

"I was hoping we could go somewhere, maybe get a coffee." She had no such intention but she needed him out of here, away from his roommate.

"Let me grab my boots," Evan said. As he walked away, she couldn't help sizing him up in the worn, soft-looking jeans that hugged his thighs and butt.

Selena had had boyfriends before, and she'd had good-looking boyfriends, but there'd never been anyone who was anything like Evan. Just looking at him made her feel all shaky inside. Seeing him *here,* where she'd seen every last inch of him, touched all of him...

"Let's go," Evan said, pulling a dark blue sweatshirt over his head. As she walked out in front of him, she felt the heat of his hand on the small of her back. Instead of leaning into it as she would've liked, she hurried down the flight of stairs to the ground floor, out of his reach.

"Where would you like to go?" he asked.

"Nowhere. I mean, not a public place. Somewhere private."

Evan grinned. "If I remember correctly, that got us into trouble the last time."

He had no idea.

She led the way to her Saturn and unlocked it with the remote. She climbed into the driver's seat. He hesitated briefly then opened the door and got in. "Where are you taking me?" he asked.

"It's a PG-rated excursion, if that puts your mind at ease."

"I'm not sure I want to get in, then." He was clearly joking, but that didn't stop Selena from considering a repeat of their first night together.

Oh, how she wished that's all she needed from him.

"I'd like to discuss something." She started the car and pulled out onto the street. Not wanting to dive into that conversation just yet, she hit the power to the radio and turned up the Haydn CD, making conversation awkward. There was that cowardice again. So be it.

She eventually turned into a public beach parking lot. She switched the ignition off but made no move to get out. "Is this okay?"

"Okay for what?" There was a gleam in his eye that she could see by the streetlight.

"Talking," she said firmly. Maybe they should get out and walk. Then she wouldn't be so overwhelmed by him, wouldn't be trapped in a small space with his very large, masculine presence. "Or we can walk."

"Here's fine. The wind is wicked on the beach to-night."

She turned toward him, pulling her right leg up on the leather seat. "This is awkward." She ran her finger back and forth over the seam on her jeans.

"What's going on?"

She met his gaze in the darkness, able to see his confusion, the gleam gone now.

"The first thing I want to say is that I've never gone home with someone I just met before. I want to make sure you understand that."

He smiled. "I'm flattered."

She didn't smile and he seemed to sense she was in dead-serious mode.

"I get that about you, Selena. I could tell. And you mentioned it about forty times that night, as well."

Now her lips did curve upward slightly. "So I did. Sorry about that."

"No need to apologize. The night was…a good one. Very good. But you must not think so. You're awfully serious."

"It…wasn't a bad night at all." She glanced up and caught his intense gaze. Frowning, she stumbled over what to say next.

Evan lightly tweaked her chin and forced eye contact again. "Tell me what's bothering you." The tenderness in his words, his actions, struck her hard, and she sat there in silence, fighting back sudden, embarrassing tears.

She could tell by his tone he didn't have any inkling of what she was about to say to him or how his life was going to change. She wished she could prepare him somehow. Really, she did. Ease him into the truth.

"Selena? It's okay, darlin'. Talk to me."

Very quietly, she took a deep, shaky breath and closed her eyes. "It's not okay, Evan. I'm pregnant."

CHAPTER FIVE

EVAN TURNED his head to look Selena in the eye. He felt as if he was moving in slow motion, as if life was happening through a thick, colorless, syruplike substance.

"Pregnant," he repeated stupidly. Did she mean…?

"Yes. Pregnant." Selena's voice was firm, confident. "I haven't slept with anyone else in a long time."

"No," he said. It couldn't be true. "We were careful."

"I thought so, too, but there must've been a problem with a condom somewhere along the line. We, um, used several…"

He remembered. Remembered well. "You're sure? I mean that you're pregnant?"

She nodded. "Believe me, I wanted the negative as much as you. More than."

"Dammit."

This wasn't supposed to happen. He was always careful. He wasn't stupid. And he sure as hell wasn't up for parenthood.

The air in the SUV felt thick and stale. Suffocating. He opened the door and got out quickly. Made his way to the beach. Vaguely, he heard the other car door slam. Selena's shoes clicked along the pavement and became silent as soon as she hit the sand. He could sense her approaching, though he didn't look at her.

What could he say?

"Evan."

She was by his side, touching his forearm.

"What's going through your head?" she asked quietly.

Something inside him snapped. "What's going through my head?" He pulled his arm away and put distance between them. "What's going through my head is that this wasn't supposed to happen. I'm not ready for it. Can't handle it. Hell, Selena, if I wanted a family, I would pursue one. Fall in love with a woman, ask her to marry me. Maybe think about kids."

He saw her take a step back as if he'd slapped her. It only registered on the surface of his brain, though. He was engrossed in the ramifications of her pregnancy.

"Ditto on all points," she said in a wavering voice. "We barely know each other. I get that. I have no idea whether we could make a go of it together if we even wanted to try."

She faltered and Evan made a point of not looking at her. She was upset? Well, so was he.

"I'm not trying to trap you. I've known for all of four days and I'm still trying to figure out what to do."

"Are you considering ending the pregnancy?" He didn't have the fortitude to examine his deep feelings on that, but the idea of making it all go away did appeal to him.

"No." Her answer was firm. Closed to debate. "Ultimately, someday, I wanted a child. Not today. But what if this is my only chance?" She shook her head. "I can't do it."

"So then we're stuck." He heard the harshness,

the chill in his own voice but couldn't bring himself to care.

"No," she said again, and this time it was even more adamant. "If you can't handle it, I'll raise the child myself. I'll have my lawyer contact you about child support."

His entire lifestyle was in danger. His freedom, his leisure time. His income and savings. Even the damn boat. Everything he'd worked for, for almost ten years, was washing away.

"I don't know what you want me to say." How would he? He barely knew this woman.

She crossed her arms over her chest and narrowed her eyes. "All you have to do is answer one question. Do you want to be involved in this or not?"

As if it was that easy. He wasn't going to decide anything now, just after having this bomb dropped on his head. "I'm outta here." He took off in the opposite direction of the parking lot.

"That's it, then?" Selena called after him, her voice full of hostility.

"Yeah," he called over his shoulder, not stopping. "I need…" What the hell did he need? A do-over. A little willpower where a certain brunette was concerned. A different box of condoms.

"I'm going home," he finally said.

WELL. Selena had her unequivocal answer, then.

Evan did not want to be in the baby's life. Or hers. She'd given him an out and he'd taken it.

Her throat tightened and tears filled her eyes without her permission. If he could walk away so easily, there was no doubt it was for the best.

The wind whipped her hair across her face and sent a shiver down her spine, but she didn't turn toward the Saturn. Instead, she was drawn to the water.

The moon was hidden by clouds tonight. Very little light hit the sand, but still, she could see the white glimmer of bubbles along the waves even through her threatening tears. She removed her shoes and sank her feet into the cold sand. She walked toward the water, stopping at the edge of the dry sand and lowering herself to the ground.

Though she knew she and Evan had never had a chance at a future, she felt more alone than she'd ever been in her twenty-seven years. She glanced up and down the beach, looking for any movement, another living being, but the sand was deserted. A gust of wind hit her and she wrapped her arms around herself for warmth.

Funny how your life could get away from you and become something you never in a million years expected, all in a fit of defiance and recklessness that lasted less than twelve hours.

Selena rested her chin on her knees and gazed out into the darkness, trying to pick out the line where sea became sky. It was impossible. But because she was stubborn and was in no position to give up on what seemed impossible, she kept right on staring. She figured the longer she looked, the clearer it would become.

EVAN STORMED through the door of his apartment and barely noticed Clay on the couch watching TV. He made a beeline to the kitchen and opened the cupboard above the fridge. Vodka, gin, tequila, rum.

"Where the hell's the whiskey?" Evan hollered.

"What whiskey?"

"I don't know. Any whiskey. Or bourbon. That'd work."

Clay muted the television and sauntered into the tiny kitchen. "We don't have bourbon or whiskey. I don't drink it. Last I knew, neither do you."

"Things change," Evan said, closing the cabinet and opening the fridge. He settled for a beer. He popped the tab and downed over half the can in one go.

"What's wrong with you?" Clay asked, helping himself to a Budweiser.

Evan finished his beer and went for another. "I am screwed, man." He swallowed a gulp and heaved himself up on the countertop. "Sca-rewed."

Clay took out a bag of pretzels from one of the cabinets and ripped it open. "Why are you screwed?"

"Remember Selena?"

"If that was Selena who was just here, it's hard to forget her. What's wrong?"

"She's pregnant."

Clay swore, choosing a colorful word that was oddly appropriate for the situation.

"Exactly." Evan leaned back and purposely banged his head on the upper cabinets.

"You're sure it's yours?" Clay asked.

"She says it is. Says she hasn't been with anyone else and if I had to guess, she's telling the truth."

They sat there for a couple of minutes, saying nothing, Clay digging in for more pretzels every few seconds and Evan crushing the empty beer can in his hand.

"So what else did she say?" Clay asked in between bites.

"She asked me what I wanted."

"And?"

"I left."

"Nice."

"I needed time to think, man. What was I supposed to do? What would you do in the situation?"

"I've been in the situation."

Aw, hell. Evan had been so wrapped up in himself he hadn't even thought about that. "I forgot. Sorry. So what'd you do when she told you?"

"I don't remember exactly. It's been three years. I know I was upset. And my baby was already born."

"Did you get pissed?"

"Nah. I handled it much better."

Evan studied Clay's face and saw the corners of his lips twitch.

"Lying SOB. Give me some of those." He grabbed the pretzel bag and helped himself to a handful.

"Yep, I was pissed at the world."

Evan tried to imagine not finding out until Selena was toting around an infant. He couldn't even fathom that.

"I proposed, eventually," Clay said. "But I wouldn't advise it. You see where it got me."

Yeah. Court battles was where Clay was with his ex, even though they'd never married.

"I've got a custody appeal in right now."

"Don't take this wrong, man, but what are you going to do with a kid?"

"Raise her, I hope."

"How?"

Clay shrugged. "I don't know. But I can do better than Robin's doing. Not a doubt in my mind about that."

"You'd have to move out."

Clay laughed at that. "You don't want a three-year-old princess as a roommate?"

Evan shuddered. "I'm sure she's cute but…my lifestyle wouldn't mesh well with a kid."

"Sounds like it's time for you to change your lifestyle then, dude."

Evan muttered a stream of swearwords, hopped down from the counter, grabbed another beer and walked out the front door.

He leaned over the railing looking into the parking lot, thankful there was no one around. The spot where Selena had parked her SUV was empty. Her face filled Evan's mind. Specifically, the look on it when he'd snapped at her. He'd seen fear. Near terror, really.

And he'd walked away.

They said your real character came through when you were faced with a major crisis, and if that was true, he was a no-good lowlife. He'd taken all his shock and anger out on Selena for the few seconds he'd hung around. Then he'd walked off, right out of her life, as if he didn't have any responsibility in the whole deal.

Exactly like his father had done.

He straightened and winged the half-full beer can down one flight to the sidewalk, unsatisfied when it didn't explode. He wanted to crush something.

If there was one thing he believed in, one thing he'd sworn since he was a kid, it was that he would never, ever turn out like his father.

Evan knew his name but he'd never known the man. Never would, now, but there'd been a time when he would've given his right leg for a real dad. To have a father in his life. One who shot hoops with him in the driveway, who watched *Simpsons* episodes with him in the evening. One who gave half a damn about his family.

In his early teens, Evan had tracked his father to a prison cell. Before he could confront him, the jackass went and died. Evan had outgrown the dream of a true family and had replaced it with hatred and pity for the man who had fathered—only in the scientific sense of the word—him and his twin sister.

He wasn't going to be that man.

He couldn't allow a child to grow up daydreaming about some fantasy dad who never appeared, inventing stories for his buddies to overcompensate for the father who wasn't part of his life.

His kid wasn't ever going to feel unwanted or worthless because of a dad who wasn't involved.

And honestly? *Dammit.* He couldn't desert the woman he'd created that kid with, either. As far as Evan knew, his mother had never heard from his father again after the day he'd walked out on her—before Evan and Melanie were even born.

That was not the kind of man Evan wanted to be.

He'd gotten himself involved—with both Selena and their unborn child—so he would have to step up. No matter how tempting it'd been to walk away.

Evan climbed up on the railing and sat on it, his feet hanging high above the first-floor sidewalk.

He had to marry Selena. They'd make a family together, bring up the child as a team. Marriage was the last thing he'd been looking for, but if he had to be trapped into one, he could do a lot worse than Selena— whose last name he still didn't know. They definitely didn't lack in chemistry, and he suspected she had a level head on her shoulders.

Determination pounded through him, along with the firm belief that this was the right thing to do.

In the morning, he had to start a twenty-four-hour shift at the station, but as soon as he finished it, he'd pay her a visit. Apologize. Ask her to marry him.

CHAPTER SIX

ART WAS Selena's refuge. Her own personal psychotherapy. Always had been. When life got tough to handle, she spent more and more time painting.

Lord knew she needed a super dose of therapy right now.

Even better, today's intense session of sketches for the city murals and beginning a new, moody acrylic of a lone fishing boat was doing double duty as earning a living. Or at least working toward such an end.

She'd worked in her studio until the sun set and then emerged from her cozy, if in need of TLC, beach house to grab a greasy tenderloin sandwich and fries from the pub three blocks west. Wrapped up in thoughts of her work, she hadn't realized a bank of clouds had blown in, and on the way home, a cold drizzle had started to fall.

When she walked in the door of the beach house, she went directly to the fireplace and stacked the wood she'd picked up the other day, as she remembered her dad doing. It took a while for the big logs to catch, but she knelt on the floor in front of the fire, poking it, mesmerized by the palette of oranges and yellows in the flames and embers. As soon as heat emanated from her respectable fire, her lids grew heavy, her eleven-hour workday catching up with her.

She lay down on the couch, perpendicular to the fireplace, and pulled the fleece throw blanket from the back of it over her. As she drifted to sleep, images of Evan found their way into her mind.

Her dreams were filled with unrest, stress. An angry man who wanted nothing to do with her. Even in sleep, she wanted to lash out, scream, remind the world, or maybe just the man, that winding up pregnant wasn't her first choice, either. Everything was wrong. Off somehow. Although she was only partially cognizant, that discordant feeling gradually overtook the anger, eating away at her, worrying her sleep until she started to wake up.

Then Selena realized it wasn't just in her dreams where something was extremely wrong. A rumbling, crackling sound filled the room, as if someone was shaking out a heavy blanket repeatedly. Frequent pops and snaps added to the noise.

Her eyes popped open and all her senses were barraged by the impending danger. Thick smoke was quickly filling the room.

She jumped up, swearing, looking frantically around and trying to gather her wits enough to figure out what to do. The curtains at the sliding glass door were burning, and the chair next to it. Black smoke dried her throat and nose. For all of two seconds, she wondered if she could throw a pan of water on the flames and put them out, but then she realized it was beyond that. She ran to the island in the kitchen and grabbed her purse, praying her cell phone was in it, then shot out the door and down the flight of stairs to the driveway.

Her heart raced and she was in enough of a panic that she struggled to dial 911. Finally, she managed it, gave the dispatcher her address and tried to answer his questions. Before they broke the connection, an engine rounded the corner down the block.

As she watched the truck pull up to the curb, she shivered and pulled the hood of her sweatshirt over her head against the light rain, huddling away from the noise of the rig and keeping her distance from the house.

A firefighter in full gear hurried out of the passenger side of the truck and gave the house a once-over from this angle. Two other men followed and immediately started grabbing equipment while the first talked into his radio to, she assumed, the dispatcher. He reported that engine one had arrived and there was smoke showing from the rear of a three-story stucco structure. He said some other things she didn't catch and that they would be entering through the front door.

Selena's heart raced, and she tried to imagine doing their job. Walking into a burning house. No thank you.

"Are all people and pets out of the house?" the firefighter asked her as he approached.

Selena nodded.

"Can you tell me where the fire is? What's burning?"

"The living room on the back side," Selena said shakily. "In that corner of the main level." She pointed to the left end of the house. "Up that flight of stairs. The curtains and a chair were burning."

"You stay here," he said. "Don't go back in the house for any reason until we give you the okay." He went back on his radio and repeated what she'd told him.

She nodded again, finding that easier than trying to be heard over the roar of the truck, and sat on the ground, hoping to catch less of the wind that way. She moved over so the engine blocked some of it and curled into her jacket, longing for the blanket she'd been wrapped in, the blanket that was probably charbroiled by now.

The firefighter who'd spoken to her quickly conferred with the others and they carried a hose to the house. They disappeared through the door where light smoke was starting to appear.

Selena's throat felt swollen and scratchy, making it difficult to swallow. What if the place blew up? Burned to the ground? She could only see a little black smoke on this side, but that could change at any second, couldn't it?

Losing the house her father had loved so much would break her. She felt closest to him here and couldn't stand to see his dream disappear. Besides, she truly didn't have anywhere else to go. This was it, and her own carelessness was to blame if the house was destroyed.

Even though one of the firefighters was still nearby, working things on the truck, she guessed, Selena felt completely alone. She didn't even have Macey's phone number, she realized. She could call her mom....

No. What good would that do? How could her mother help her from Boston? She wasn't about to go crying home, not until she absolutely had to. Maybe the fire would be extinguished before much damage was done.

Several people from surrounding vacation houses and condos had begun to gather around her property. Selena had never met any of them and didn't want to now. She made a point of avoiding eye contact and huddled even deeper into herself.

Tears filled her eyes and she stared at the house,

expecting to see the orange lick of devouring flames any second. When she couldn't stand it any longer, she dialed information on her phone to find the number of Macey's bar. When she finally got through, she was told Macey wasn't currently working. She explained in a rush what was happening and the man promised he would try to track Macey down for her.

Selena buried her face in her legs and let the tears pour out.

EVAN HAD BEEN on the nozzle and he'd been able to put the fire down fast. Cleanup, however, was taking three times as long. They'd ventilated the house, removed the charred pieces and cleaned up the water, among other routine postfire tasks.

At last, Evan helped the others haul equipment to the engine and stowed everything in its place. He took off his helmet and ran his hand through his hair, wishing that could get rid of the stink of smoke. Captain Mendoza went over to talk to the occupant, a woman who looked to be soaked to the bone in a hooded sweatshirt. Her shoulders drooped and her head hung low as Captain Mendoza spoke to her.

He could understand how having a fire in your house would be overwhelming and scary as hell, but truthfully this woman was lucky. The fire had been slow to spread and there wasn't a lot of damage beyond the living room. The sliding glass door had been blown out and she'd need a professional service to restore the rest of the room, but beyond that, the main problem would be the smell. The ritzy beach house would likely be habitable soon.

The purse that the woman clung to caught his attention—he'd seen it somewhere before. He swore to himself as he realized when and where: last night, on the floor between the front seats of Selena's SUV.

He looked closer and the hair that fell out of the sides of the wet hood was dark and wavy and below her shoulders. Now that he stared, he recognized that stance, the long legs, the curve of her hips.

He moved toward her without a second thought.

"Selena?"

Her head jerked toward him, and he could tell she was just as surprised to see him.

"Evan?" Her gaze roved quickly up and down him.

"Are you okay?" He lowered his eyes to her abdomen.

She nodded as tears started falling down her face. Hell. He moved past the captain and put an arm around her. When she buried her face in the rough, dirty sleeve of his coat, he instinctively pulled her to him.

Captain Mendoza gave him a questioning look. Evan nodded once and the captain walked off toward the truck.

He could feel Selena's jerky intakes of breath, telling him she was crying, but she kept it silent. Captain Mendoza returned and handed him a thick blanket from the rig and Evan thanked him.

"Let's put this around you," he said gently. "You're shivering."

She didn't argue, just looked at him with sad eyes as he unfolded the blanket and wrapped it around her shoulders.

"I know you're upset, darlin', but are you physically okay? Did you take in any smoke?"

Selena shook her head. "I don't think so. I'm fine."

He didn't have to fake his concern and pulled her to him again, tucking her head under his chin. "What happened? Do you know?"

SELENA SUCKED IN a deep breath and straightened, putting space between them. She'd been so surprised to see him, and feeling so alone and scared, that she'd gone to him like a puppy. Now that she'd cried all over him, she could more easily recall the way he'd reacted to her news, treated her.

"I started a fire in the fireplace," she said just loud enough to be heard over the engine. "I was beat and I guess I fell asleep on the couch."

"No more fires when you're so tired." He rubbed her upper arm through the blanket, but if his intent was tenderness, Selena overlooked it.

"What does it matter to you?"

"Selena, I'm sorry about last night. We need to talk but this isn't the place."

A nod was all she could manage. She was bone tired, totally spent. Couldn't even think about the drama between them.

"I work till morning. Can we talk tomorrow sometime?"

"Whenever." She wasn't about to be easy on him now. Not after the night she'd spent alone, terrified, angry.

"Do you have a place to go tonight?" Evan asked.

"Taken care of," she lied. It would be, soon enough. Macey was on her way and she'd either stay with her or get a cheap hotel room.

"How'd you score such a nice rental, anyway?" he asked, sizing up the house, which showed no damage on this side. A little worse for wear from age and neglect, it still looked majestic, especially with its turret room and widow's walk.

Selena swallowed, determined to keep her family's money out of this. "I know the owner."

"Will he put you up somewhere else? Another rental?"

"It's all taken care of," she said again. "Looks like you better go." She glanced around him to the three other firefighters, who were still cleaning up.

"I'm not going to walk off and leave you here by yourself."

"You did last night."

She couldn't help it. He'd hurt her and she wasn't over it yet.

She could almost hear him counting to ten. "I said I'm sorry. I don't know what else I can do right now but I want to discuss everything. Later. When I'm not working, smelling like smoke."

A red pickup truck pulled up behind the fire engine. Macey descended from the passenger side and jogged over to Selena.

"Are you okay?" Macey threw her arms around her as if they'd been friends since preschool.

Selena could finally smile genuinely in spite of the day, the fire. "I'm fine. The house will be okay with a little work. You didn't have to rush over here."

"You tell me the house is on fire, I'm supposed to sit at home and watch a movie?" Macey finally released her and noticed Evan, who'd walked over to talk to the guy who'd arrived in the truck with Macey—Selena assumed it was her fiancé. "Evan? Everything under control?"

"Didn't realize you two knew each other," Evan said, not hiding his surprise.

The other guy shrugged and looked at Macey.

"I could say the same," Macey said, her gaze darting between Selena and Evan.

"We've met and Evan was just telling me he has to get back to work," Selena said, hoping to steer Macey toward her truck.

Evan stared at her, clearly wanting to say more but settling for one word. "Tomorrow."

"Later, Drake," the other guy said as he went toward the driver's side.

"Selena, this is my fiancé, Derek Severson. He's a firefighter, too."

"Nice to meet you," she said automatically.

"You're coming with us," Macey said.

Her blood chilled at the thought of marrying a man in that kind of dangerous job.

Oh God.

She'd been in such a daze it only just now hit her. The father of her baby was in *exactly* that dangerous job.

Nausea doubled her over and her head swam.

"Selena?" Macey came up beside her and supported her arm as they got to the truck. "What's wrong, hon?"

Selena breathed in fresh, wet air, trying to regain her equilibrium. She shook her head. "I'm okay. Just absorbing everything, I guess."

Which was true. Absorbing it as much as she could. She'd promised herself for so long that she'd never get involved with someone who risked his life on a daily basis. She couldn't have gone out and handpicked someone who scared her more.

CHAPTER SEVEN

IT COULDN'T BE this hard to change a lightbulb. Could it?

Selena knew full well she was *challenged* when it came to everyday household tasks. Not something she was proud of, but when you had a staff to change light-bulbs and vacuum the carpets, why would you insist on doing it yourself? It hadn't ever crossed her mind.

She wasn't complaining. She was lucky to have been left this house in her dad's will. Even luckier to be back in it twenty-four hours after the fire. The damage wasn't too bad—she'd already had a restoration company out as well as a contractor to give her an estimate on the boarded-up glass door, thanks to Derek's help. Some of the furniture and decor from the living room had to be trashed but those were just things. The biggest prob-lem was the smoke stench, but she had all the windows on the main floor open, ceiling fans running, and had moved in extra fans to push fresh air through, as well. Some of her wardrobe would likely have to go, but it wouldn't fit for much longer anyway.

She stretched up to the ceiling of her studio again, standing on tiptoe on the arm of the overstuffed chair she'd pushed to the middle of the room. She and the beach house didn't seem to own a ladder. Daylight brightened this room whether the sun shone or not, but to handle the murals and her start-up business, SJ Enterprises, she planned to put in work after the sun went down. The dim bulb that'd been here wasn't at all sufficient.

It'd taken her ages to unscrew the heavy glass cover of the light and then it had slipped out of her hands and fallen. Thankfully the cover had hit the cushioned chair—barely—instead of shattering on the hardwood.

Lowering her arms and moving closer to the now-empty socket, she turned her iPod up as high as it would go, trying to lose herself in the music. She stretched up yet again and made another attempt. It didn't seem like the bulb would ever fit, but what did she know? She could barely reach the socket.

When a man suddenly appeared in the doorway from the stairs, Selena screamed and dropped the lightbulb. It took her a split second to realize it was Evan. His eyes widened.

The bulb hit the chair cushion, rolled off and shattered.

She yanked her earbuds out and left them dangling. "What are you doing here?"

Beyond the surprise of an intruder, her heart raced in a dozen different directions. Sure, he'd said he wanted to talk, but she wasn't the type to believe a man who said that. Especially not one who'd reacted so badly just two days ago.

"Making sure you don't kill yourself changing a lightbulb, it appears. Don't move." He came into the room, glanced around and picked up the trash basket next to her plastic art supply cart. "Do you have a broom?"

Selena laughed hollowly. "A broom? Not to my knowledge." She started to climb down.

"I said don't move." Evan plucked the glass shards off the floor and tossed them into the trash. "How did the chair get there?"

"I pushed it." She couldn't prevent the "duh" tone.

He stood and met her eyes. "You are not supposed to be moving heavy furniture."

"Says who?"

"Me."

"And why would I do anything you say?"

"Because you're carrying my child."

She sat down heavily on the cushion. Since when did he consider the baby his child? "Last I knew it was relegated to being *my* child. How did you get in here?"

"I walked. You should lock your door."

"I thought I did when the contractor left."

"Opened right up." Evan double-checked for glass shards on the floor then put the trash basket back where it belonged. Returning his attention to Selena, he frowned. "You're a tough woman to find."

"I've been here for hours. I had a restoration company in here for most of the day."

"Didn't think you'd be back here so fast. Figured the owner would want to make repairs before letting you in."

"The owner's fine with it. I went to Derek and Macey's place. Left there early this morning." She crawled over the arm of the chair to the floor. He was looming too close and she didn't like feeling trapped. She began pushing the chair to its original place.

"Dammit, Selena. Do you listen?"

"Only when it suits me. There's no reason I can't push this back. It slides easily enough."

He removed her hands and finished the job for her.

"Why do you think it's okay to barge into my home?" she said, scowling at his back while not allowing her gaze to stray too low.

"You didn't answer when I knocked or rang the bell."

"That doesn't make it okay to come on in."

He held up his hand. "Look, Selena, I don't apologize much, let alone multiple times for the same offense, but I'm sorry for the other night. I didn't handle the news well."

"No, you didn't."

"I was caught completely off guard."

"You said an apology, not excuses."

He looked away, clearly frustrated.

"So you've apologized. Now you can go."

Evan shook his head. "We're going to talk."

She really wanted to kick him out and not hear anything he had to say. What was the point? She could never have a future with him. He might be a nice guy; maybe he was a warm, caring person, but she couldn't—wouldn't—let her child live with the fear of losing him. Selena knew that fear too well.

Going through it again would wreck her almost as much as watching her son or daughter suffer it.

The sun was sinking quickly. She turned on the lamp on the end table, then sank into the chair's big cushions, tucking her legs beneath her. Fatigue rolled over her as it seemed to do every day lately. It was all she could do to hold her head up and look at him. "Say what you came to say."

Evan perched on the stool in front of her easel. His face was etched with worry, shoulders rigid. He studied the paint she'd spattered on the floor, his fingers steepled on his thighs.

Selena allowed herself to admire those large, capable hands, a little awed in spite of herself. Those hands had the power to save buildings, rescue people, and yet they could be so tender on a woman's body.

"I… We should get married," Evan said finally, meeting her gaze head-on.

There was a two-second lapse as his words sank in and she switched gears from the hot memory of the night they'd shared to the icy fear of having him in her life.

"Why would we do that?" she blurted. "You seemed content to stay out of it the other night."

"Knee-jerk reaction."

"You don't have to marry me, Evan. This isn't the fifties."

"I do. It's my child as much as yours."

Selena chewed frantically on her lip. "We aren't getting married."

"You haven't even considered it."

She popped off the chair and walked to the row of windows that overlooked the water. "I don't need to consider it. The answer is no."

"This is my child, too. We make decisions together. You don't get to say no."

"About marrying you? Oh, yes, I do."

"So you're fine with making our child's life a nightmare just like that?" he asked.

"It's more likely it would be a nightmare if we *did* get married."

"Do you really want to get into splitting custody? I

get the kid on days A, B and C and you get him on D, E and F? Two beds, two wardrobes, two toy boxes?"

"Are you saying you want custody?" A new fear niggled at her. She'd barely started to brew this baby and they were already arguing about custody? That was another slice of life she'd prefer her child to avoid.

"I'm saying I want to do this together. In the same house."

"So we get married for show?"

He came up behind her and brushed her hair back behind her shoulder. His breath caressed the side of her neck.

"There's a lot more between us than that," he said in a near-whisper. "The way I remember it, we didn't have any trouble making things work in the bedroom."

His words sent unwanted heat through her. Dammit. "So we share a house and have unlimited sex. Sounds like a great deal for a kid."

"Better than the alternative." He pivoted away from her and took over the chair. When she turned to look at him, his forehead rested on his hands and he rubbed his temples.

"What changed, Evan? The other night you were hell-bent on not having anything to do with me or the pregnancy. Now, two days later you want the complete opposite?"

She could see his jaw tighten, even across the dimly lit room. He didn't meet her eyes. Selena walked over to him as calmly as she could and sat on the fat arm of the chair since there was no other comfortable place to sit. "Explain it to me," she said. "Because for all I know, tomorrow you'll be back to 'no way, I'm outta here.'"

He merely shook his head. "I won't change my mind. You can count on it."

"Neither will I."

"You won't even consider marrying me?"

"No."

He stood, punching the other arm of the chair. He paced to the far wall and back again, then stared down at her. "Why?"

He would never understand her fears about his job if she told him, just as her mother didn't truly grasp the way her brother's special ops career made her feel. They thought she was overreacting, being a spoiled brat.

Selena just shook her head.

Evan stared at her for a long moment. "Unfortunately, I'm stubborn when I don't get my way. I'm not giving up on this, Selena. I *will* be in this child's life. And I'm going to make you see that marrying me is the best thing for us."

"Good luck," she said.

"Why the hell did you tell me about the pregnancy if you don't want me to have any part in this child's life?" Evan demanded.

She hadn't known a thing about him then. Like, oh, his career. His calling. "I couldn't not tell you," she fibbed. "I guess I hoped…"

"You hoped I'd be a jackass and walk away."

"Yes." She sat up taller and braced herself to keep lying. "That's what I hoped then. And what I still do."

"You're going to be sadly disappointed then, darlin'."

There was nothing she could say back to him. All she could do was hope that he got over this he-man, you're-mine phase quickly. He could pester her all he wanted, but she was not going to cave. She wouldn't marry Evan Drake, no matter how sexy and kind he was. Because he was so sexy and kind. She wouldn't let herself love the man.

CHAPTER EIGHT

"THERE ARE two hot women over there," Derek said from behind the bar at the Shell Shack. "You haven't said a word to them. What gives?"

Evan craned his neck to see what he was yammering about. "Not bad from this angle," he said of the two blondes facing away from them. He shrugged and turned back around. He and Clay had come in for dinner and a beer and, for once, that's really all he wanted.

"Not bad?" The old man sitting two seats over harrumphed loudly.

"You remember my uncle Gus," Derek said.

Evan nodded and waved. "I know Gus. You can have dibs this time, man."

"You don't usually share, the way I remember it. Besides, I got my own woman now."

"Where is Thelma?" Derek asked. "She kick you out?"

"She's getting her hair curled, boy. Thought I'd use the opportunity to make sure you're not still screwing this place up. So what's got you in such a dither?" He directed the latter to Evan.

Clay glanced sideways at Evan, no doubt womdering if he was going to come clean.

"Gus, did it occur to you that maybe it's none of your business?" Derek asked.

"It's fine," Evan said. "Going to get around anyway." He paused to take a drink. "I got a girl pregnant."

"Hoo, dog." Gus got down from his place and moved to a closer stool.

Derek stared at him. "It's you?"

"What's me?"

"You and Selena? Macey told me about Selena's... predicament but I don't think she knows that morsel. Whoa." Derek refilled Evan's and Clay's drinks.

Evan didn't say anything. Didn't need to. "How did she and Macey become so tight, anyway?"

"They met here at the bar. Apparently became best friends forever immediately. You know how chicks are. Selena told her."

"Hell. Was I the last to know?" Evan asked.

"Don't get your sexy *Playgirl* briefs in a twist. She didn't say it was you."

Evan closed his eyes, still not used to his new reality. "It's me."

"What are you going to do about the kid?" Gus asked.

Evan shoved the last of his fries in his mouth and chewed while the three men stared at him impatiently. He and Clay hadn't discussed the subject since Evan had slammed out the door the other night. "I asked Selena to marry me."

Clay set his beer down hard. "You did what?"

"Are you nuts?" Derek asked.

"That's my boy," Gus said triumphantly.

"Marriage is good enough for you," Evan said to Derek. "Why not me?"

"Call me old-fashioned, but you don't even know this woman, do you?"

"I know her intimately," Evan said, smiling.

Gus hooted. "That warrants a round on the house!" He slid his empty cup toward Derek.

"You're done, old man," Derek told him as he tossed the cup into the trash.

"You're making a mistake, Evan," Clay said.

"You think I shouldn't get involved?"

"Something tells me it doesn't matter what I think." Clay threw his napkin into his empty burger basket.

"Exactly." Now that he'd made up his mind, Evan wouldn't be swayed, no matter who tried to do the swaying. "End of conversation."

"Man knows what he wants," Gus said. "Y'all should respect that."

"Aren't you supposed to be picking up a boat this weekend?" Derek took the empty baskets from Clay and Evan and set them on the back counter.

Evan swigged more beer. "Boat's off. I'm going to need that money to support Selena and the baby."

"Judging by the house she's living in, she doesn't need your money," Clay said. "Thing's a freaking mansion."

"She knows the owner. I don't think she's paying for it."

"She doesn't give off the poor-chick vibe if you ask me," Clay said.

"So you're giving up your yacht just like that?" Derek asked. "Something you haven't shut up about since I met you? Out the window?"

"It sucks, man, but this is something I have to do. As much as I want that thing, I can't justify it. That boat would take up a big chunk of my savings and, last I knew, kids cost money."

"Almost as much as women," Derek said drily.

"I can see holding off on the boat," Clay weighed in. "I just think it'd be wise to do the same with the wedding bells."

"Says the guy who immediately proposed when he found out he had a child." Evan shook his head in disbelief. "You were already long broken up if I remember the story right."

"Thank God she turned me down."

"You think this woman's going to go along with your grand plan?" Derek asked.

Evan sucked down the rest of his beer. "I reckon it'll take some time to convince her."

"She said no," Clay guessed.

"So far. I plan to change her mind. You guys know I have a stubborn side."

"About the size of the Atlantic," Clay said. "More power to you. Hope it works out somehow."

"Woman's a fool if she doesn't change her mind," Gus said.

"Do you actually get paid for standing around talking to your friends?" Macey, full of her usual energy, headed straight for Derek with a wide, flirty grin.

Evan watched Derek embrace her and Macey reach up and kiss him.

"Wages around here stink, anyway," Derek said, bending down to kiss her again, this time longer. "Boss is a slave driver."

"Do you mind? I'm trying to digest here," Evan said.

"Sore loser." Derek was obviously referring yet again to the one date Evan had taken Macey out on. One time.

Actually it wasn't even worthy of being called a date, because Macey had been hung up on Derek even then.

"Hey, Gus," Macey said when she noticed him. "Thelma let you out to play today?"

"I go out whenever I want to," the old man corrected her. "With a woman like her, I don't much want to."

The guys chuckled and Macey shook her head.

Gus glanced at his watch. "Fact, she oughta be home now. Think I'll go join her. Good to see you, Macey Girl."

"You, too, Gus." They said goodbye and watched him totter off toward the bus stop.

"Evan, tell Macey your news so I don't have to," Derek said.

Evan leveled a frown at his friend. "Please. Be my guest."

"What? Somebody tell me." Macey looked from one to the other, waiting for someone to spill it.

"Evan's going to be a papa," Derek said.

Her eyes widened and Evan saw the moment when she put one and one together and came up with three. "She never mentioned your name."

"Now you know."

"The other night at the fire…that makes more sense now." Macey leaned against Derek as if they were both more comfortable together than apart. "In all the chaos I forgot to bring it up."

"Did you hear the latest?" Derek asked her. "Evan proposed."

Macey sobered. "You asked her to marry you?"

"I did."

"Don't worry," Clay said. "She turned him down."

Macey stepped up to the bar and leaned over the counter toward him. "You? Married?"

"Apparently not yet," Evan replied. "I would've thought you might be on my side."

"I'm not taking sides. I just want both of you to do whatever's going to work in the long run."

"I think marriage is it. So tell me. How do I change her mind?"

Macey tapped the counter thoughtfully. "Give her some time. Let her get to know you."

"That'll scare her away for good," Derek said.

"Guys, give him a break. He's trying to do the right thing." Macey scowled at her fiancé.

"Yes, ma'am," Derek said.

She deepened her frown, making Derek smile.

"You're right," he said. "I wish the best for you, dude. Whatever that is."

"So tell us about this girl," Clay said to Macey. "Evan doesn't know much other than what she looks like naked."

That wasn't all, but Evan wasn't about to share some of the things he *did* learn during their night together. He attempted to act nonchalant, but the truth was that he wanted to hear whatever Macey would tell.

"She's an artist," Macey said. "A really talented one. And she's going into business, so you guys should all buy her stuff once it's available. She's doing the city murals, too. Including one at the station."

"So she's staying around?" Evan said.

Macey raised her brows smugly, which she did a lot, but always got away with because she smiled at the same time. "If I didn't know better, I'd think you might be trolling for info."

"Maybe," Evan admitted.

"We need to know if this woman is someone Evan can trust," Clay added. "The times I've seen her she's so preoccupied with Daddy-O here, she barely says two words to me."

"Selena has a great personality."

"Aww, don't tell them that," Evan said. "You don't do her justice."

"It's the truth. She's supernice and…" Macey peered at Evan thoughtfully. "And that's all I'm going to tell you. If you want to know more, you can ask her. Get to know her yourself. I'm not your spy." Again with the smug smile.

"I intend to try," Evan said. "But there are two problems. One, I doubt she'll willingly answer, and two, I still haven't managed to get her phone number. Maybe you could help me with the second one."

He ignored the howls from Clay and Derek and slid a clean napkin in front of Macey. Reaching over the counter, he grabbed a pen from the nearby cash register and handed it to her. She looked at him but didn't move.

"That's fine," he said, raising his hands. "You go ahead and be difficult, *Mrs. Derek*. I can work around you."

Macey laughed. She picked up the pen and wrote a number on the napkin. "I have no doubt in my mind that you can, so I'll save you some time. But you'll have to convince her to see you on your own. Delve deep into that well of charm."

Evan took the napkin from her and tucked it into his back pocket. He threw some bills on the counter and stood. "I'm outta here."

"Good luck, man," Clay said.

"Tell her you're giving up your lifelong dream of owning a boat," Derek suggested. "Maybe that'll make her see you're serious."

Everyone had advice. If he thought any of it would work, he'd try it, because Selena was possibly the biggest challenge he'd ever faced. It might take all nine months of her pregnancy, but he would wear her down. Somehow.

CHAPTER NINE

EVAN HAD been mulling for days now how a guy was supposed to get someone to marry him when she never answered his phone calls or called him back.

No more trying to talk to Selena on the phone. He'd come to the station to request vacation time in a few weeks, but he'd also hoped she would be out front working on the mural as she'd done yesterday when he was on duty. Once he'd spotted her, he hadn't had the opportunity to go out to her right away, and by the time he did, she'd quit for the day. Today, he intended to surprise her.

Evan entered the conference room, which had the clearest view of the front courtyard and the mural outside. Sure enough, he spotted her standing on the opposite side of the curved wall, deep in concentration. He admired her silky dark hair, pulled into a sloppy ponytail, and was amused by how she stuck out the tip of her tongue to the side as she worked.

His hand was already wrapped around his cell phone, since he'd checked for messages as he'd walked out of the admin office. Evan punched in Selena's number from memory and hit Send. Then he moved nearer to the windows to catch her in the act of blowing him off yet again.

The only clue that the call went to the correct phone

was the distracted movement of her head—she switched her focus from the wall to something on the ground a few feet away—for a fraction of a second. He knew her phone had to be lying there even though the four-foot-high wall blocked his view.

The call went through to voice mail, where he once again got a recording saying she wasn't available. She looked pretty available to him. He disconnected and crossed his arms, watching her work again. Thirty seconds later, he hit Redial.

This time she didn't even glance sideways when the ringing started. Evan stalked to the entrance foyer and went straight out the door toward her, his phone still pressed to his ear. He heard ringing in stereo as he drew nearer to her, but Selena didn't even notice him.

Voice mail again, of course. This time he left a message.

"You know, it's mighty rude to ignore a guy time after time when he calls," he said into the phone.

Selena turned her head sharply in his direction. Their eyes met but he kept talking, still recording as if he wasn't standing ten feet away from her.

"I've called you several dozen times now and while most men would take your silence as a rejection, you're not so lucky with me. So I'm going to keep trying and hope you take pity on me real soon."

Evan ended the call and raised his eyebrows as he looked at her.

"I was trying to get this part of the sketch just right," she explained. Lamely, in his opinion.

"What about the other thirty-seven times I've called in the past couple of days?"

She smiled sheepishly. "Was that you? I'm sorry. I didn't recognize the number."

"You don't lie very well."

He walked around the wall to see her work. A lightly sketched collage was beginning to take shape across the entire twenty feet of surface. It appeared to be a sketch of firefighters fighting a big blaze in a large building. He thought he recognized it from the coverage of the hotel fire four or five years ago. "Looking good."

"It'll get there," she said, eyeing it critically.

"You think if you ignore me I'll go away?" he asked in a friendly tone.

Her shoulders sagged. "Hoping?"

"You seemed to like me that first night."

Selena stared at the ground. "It's not that I don't like you. I don't really know you. I just..." She shrugged. "I'm not going to marry you, Evan."

"Scared?"

"No."

"You're afraid if you spend any time with me at all, you'll fall head over heels in love. Then you'll be begging me to marry you."

"Dream on."

"Have dinner with me."

"I'm working."

Evan glanced at the sky. "The sunlight isn't optimal."

"Are you an artist now?" she asked.

"No, but I can see the light out here will suck in about ten minutes."

"Yeah." Selena looked at the sky and frowned. "I'm almost done for the day."

"I'll wait for you and then we can go grab some food."

She turned her head to him again. "I never agreed to a date."

"Not a date. Just nourishment. You have to eat."

"I'm covered with paint and grime. I'd rather go home."

"Tell you what. You finish up here while I go get some food. I'll deliver."

"You don't play fair." She didn't seem particularly thrilled, but that was okay. He'd change her mind about their future, one gray-matter cell at a time.

"Where's your SUV?"

"I walked."

"I'll pick you up, then."

"I don't know what you expect, but I'm exhausted," she said, bending to put some of her supplies in a large plastic box.

"I expect you to eat enough for two people. I'll be back in fifteen."

He walked away before she had a chance to protest further.

SELENA RUSHED through her shower instead of lingering in the hot water as she longed to do. Having Evan in her kitchen made her antsy. Oh, who was she fooling? Having him in the same latitude made her downright nervous.

At times in his presence, all she could think about was the night they'd been together. There were moments when she could fool herself into believing they'd known each other for much longer than they actually had. But then he'd look at her a certain way and her stomach would flutter and flip, driving home that she was having a baby with a stranger. A disturbingly hot one, at that.

She finished drying off and told herself that searching for her light yellow lace bra—which was fast becoming too small—and matching panties was just maintaining the status quo, not an attempt to be sexy. To compensate, she pulled on old leggings she'd decorated with paint and her favorite pink zip-up hoodie. Just an everyday dinner in her everyday beach house with an everyday guy.

Right. Except Mr. Everyday looked like God's answer to Angelina Jolie and, oh, she happened to be carrying his child.

Selena sat on the bed.

Her stomach growled; she was bordering on nausea. He had food—she could smell it from here.

She dried her hair and skipped makeup. If she didn't get some food now, she might pass out.

Evan presided over the table. In front of him was a loaded double cheeseburger, large fries and a drink big enough to correct a national drought. Selena's place setting held noticeably less food.

"A salad and a little kid's milk?" she asked, trying to hide her panic that she would never get full.

"It's a big salad," he said. "I did my best to keep it healthy for you. I'm sure you don't want a bunch of grease and fat."

Okay, his intentions were thoughtful, but…

"You said it yourself, I'm eating for two."

"I should've ordered a second salad," Evan said.

"Plus a burger and fries. Don't take this the wrong way but I could eat a truck."

His eyes roved over her body and she didn't miss his appreciation. "Where are you going to put all that?"

Her hand automatically went to her abdomen. "In here. Thank you for trying to keep it healthy, but I'm going to run and get myself more. Sometimes grease is necessary." Her purse and cell phone were on the counter and she went toward them.

"Sit, Selena. You can have my food."

"What are you going to eat?"

"I'll start with your healthy salad unless you're dying to eat it."

She shook her head.

"And then I'll get more when I take you out for ice cream afterward."

"I don't need ice cream."

"Do you like it?" he asked.

"Of course, but..."

"Pregnant women are supposed to eat lots of ice cream. I'm getting you an extra-large sundae from Lambert's on the beach."

She considered arguing—their deal had only been for a quick dinner. But...ice cream. It sounded heavenly, and now that the idea was in her head, she knew she wouldn't forget about it until she satisfied the craving. "So much for healthy. I'll eat the burger. You keep the fries and salad."

"We'll split the fries."

Sitting down, she agreed.

The phone she'd left on the counter rang then—an irritating cacophony of bird tweets and squawks. She knew that ring and the one person it signaled all too well.

"I'll get that for you," Evan said.

Selena held up her hand. "Don't. It's not someone I want to talk to."

Evan was about to get up and stopped. "So I'm not the only one whose calls you ignore."

Selena busied herself scooping up an errant splatter of mayo with a fry.

"Is there anyone whose calls you actually answer?" he asked.

"A few lucky people," she said noncommittally.

"Who's the poor sucker lumped into the same category as me? A boyfriend somewhere? An ex?"

"My mother."

"Ouch."

"Don't tell me you never screen your calls," she said.

"I never screen my calls. I figure they'll just call back later. Might as well deal with it and get it over with."

"So you *do* have people you don't want to talk to."

"On occasion. Does the blowing off ever work out for you in the end?"

"What's that supposed to mean?" she asked.

"You tried to ignore me and here I am."

"I could still kick you out."

"But you won't. You want that sundae."

Selena chuckled. "You think you know all my secrets now that you've found the food button."

"I know a few of your most private secrets," he said, and the look he gave her made it clear he was referring to their night together. Her body heated up.

"I'm not marrying you."

"I've never had to feed a pregnant lady before," Evan said as if she hadn't spoken. He grinned and watched with unabashed interest as Selena stuffed the piled-high burger into her mouth.

"Me, neither," she said after chewing. "It's apparently a big job."

"Have you had morning sickness?" he asked between mouthfuls of salad.

"Only when I wake up. Crackers take care of it, though."

"The doctor said that's normal?"

"I haven't been to a doctor," Selena admitted. She'd lain awake for hours a couple of nights ago worrying about both her lack of medical care and health insurance.

"That's important, isn't it?"

"I'm going soon."

"Do you have an appointment yet?"

"What is this, twenty questions?"

"What are you hiding?"

Selena opened the squat little milk carton and drained most of it in one go. "I'm not hiding anything. I'm going to the San Amaro County health clinic next week."

"The free clinic?" Evan's disbelief startled her.

"Yes." She raised her chin a notch. She'd never been to a free health clinic in her life and no matter how hard she tried to tell herself it was fine, it was the perfect symbol of just how much her life had changed in a few weeks.

"You can't go there," Evan said.

"I can." She ate the last bite of burger before adding. "I have to."

"You should go to an obstetrician."

She'd prefer that but her days of being choosy were over. "Are you a snob?" she asked. "Free clinics have good doctors on staff. A lot of the kids I worked with in Boston went to the county health clinic and got decent medical care."

"The one here has problems. They've had trouble getting a doctor—apparently there's a shortage in this area—so they only have a nurse-practitioner most days."

"What's wrong with a nurse-practitioner?" She had a general rule of avoiding medical personnel of all kinds, but pregnancy had a way of forcing a woman to get over a medical phobia fast. Selena had already accepted that she'd have to see a lot more of doctors than she wanted for the next few months, but she wasn't sure about a nurse-practitioner. Evan made it sound scary.

"With most nurse-practitioners, nothing. I just don't care for the one in the clinic. I went to school with her and know too much about her."

Her anxiety made her feel as if her chest was closing in. She was trapped and couldn't hide the fact anymore. "I don't have money or insurance to pay for a doctor's appointment," she said breathlessly, a sheen of sweat popping out on her brow.

"If you'd marry me, you'd have the best benefits on the island."

She slid her chair back and stood. "Can we get that ice cream now? You must still be hungry."

He stared at her a moment, then wisely he stood and took his keys out of his pocket.

They threw away their trash and locked up the house. Evan opened the passenger door of his big black pickup for her and she climbed up to the seat. "Does the size of this thing ever seem like overkill?" she asked as he got in on the driver's side.

"Nah. Comes in handy."

"I imagine it's a big hit with all your legions of dates."

"What makes you think I have legions of dates?"

"Don't you?"

He turned his head to look at her and smiled. "Don't believe everything you hear."

A few minutes later, they were in the truck again with their ice cream. He'd ordered a banana split and Selena had gone for a butter pecan sundae that was as big as her head. The wind was too strong for them to enjoy their desserts outside, and she hadn't invited him back to her place, so here they sat.

"I'm going to take you to a doctor," Evan said out of nowhere.

"No."

"Why not?"

"I told you, I don't have the money."

"I'm offering to pay."

She shook her head without hesitation as she swallowed ice cream. "I can't accept that."

"Why not?"

"I hardly know you."

He stared at her. "You've seen my underwear."

She looked him in the eye, starting to grin. "And then some."

Their eyes locked for several seconds and Selena found herself picturing him out of his underwear again.

Evan brushed her hair behind her ear in a gesture that didn't feel as innocent as it should have. "It's my baby, too. I want both of you to have the best care. Let me do this."

She wasn't sure if it was the light, erotic touch of his fingers on her jaw or just a need to have someone else in on this with her, but she found herself nodding. "Just this once."

EVAN COULDN'T DENY his desire for this woman. He really needed to keep control of himself around her—coming on strong would do nothing to make her see his way about marriage—but it was as if she'd cast a spell on him. He liked being with her. Liked that she didn't pull punches. He was relieved she'd finally agreed to go to a real doctor and let him pay—he suspected that wasn't easy for her.

And damn if he didn't want to kiss her like crazy right now as she stared at him across the front seat. Her eyes glittered seductively in the moonlight, reeling him in, drawing him closer.

Selena set her sundae dish in the cup holder, and Evan brushed her hair back from her face. He ran his hand to the back of her alluring neck and pulled her lips to his.

He took in her scent—vanilla with a hint of peach—and burrowed his fingers into her soft waves. Their tongues met and the intimacy of the touch drove his desire higher. He breathed her in. Wanted to consume her. But he fought to hold himself in check. He could tell she was holding herself back, as well. Being careful.

She backed away from the contact too early, and he let her. Not because he wanted to keep it under control—it was the opposite, actually. The slightest touch from her made him crazy, brought their lovemaking back to him in an onslaught of memories. Another few seconds of kissing her wouldn't be enough.

"You didn't allow that just out of gratitude, did you?" he asked huskily.

"What if I did?" She didn't quite smile and he couldn't tell what she was thinking.

"Then I like the way you show your thanks."

"It wasn't gratitude. I'd much rather *not* be indebted to you. Just a slipup. My bad."

He wove his fingers with hers and pulled her close again, unable to resist touching her. "You aren't indebted to me, first off. And second, not a thing about that was bad."

"I don't want you to get the wrong idea. Next thing I know you'll have a preacher hired."

He chuckled. "I like to think I wouldn't have to force a woman to marry me. I have faith you'll come around."

"What'd they put in your drink?"

"Nothing, unfortunately." He leaned back in his seat to resist the very nagging temptation to taste her some more. "Selena, I like kissing you."

He could actually see her guard go up—her shoulders stiffened and all signs of levity disappeared from her face.

"That's a compliment," he said, unwilling to think about how much he wanted to put a grin back on her face.

She nodded once. She wasn't going to give him an inch.

"Maybe I'm the densest man alive, but it seems like maybe you like kissing me, too."

"Okay, yeah. I do. Until you get all cocky afterward," she said stubbornly.

"Here's the deal. Our future isn't resolved yet. That

little *M* word that sends you into orbit will come up again. But why shouldn't we let things happen as they happen?"

"Things?"

"Kissing. What have you. If you're suddenly overwhelmed by the need to crawl all over me, why not?"

Selena almost chuckled but stopped herself. "We need to work on your self-esteem, build it up so you're not so modest."

"My point is that we can kiss without having to get married. Can't we?"

"We just did." She hadn't relaxed a bit.

"Okay, then…"

"Try it again and I'll hurt you. Just because I let it happen once doesn't mean I will again."

Evan grinned and started up the truck, knowing his fun was over for the evening. "Okay, let's review," he said as he drove out of Lambert's parking lot. "Two things we've established tonight. Number one—feed the pregnant woman. Well. Two—kissing is perfectly acceptable."

"One out of two isn't bad. Then add three—drive the pregnant woman home now because she is hormonal, exhausted and not kissing anymore."

He glanced over at her and thought how pretty she looked when she copped an attitude.

Changing this woman's mind was going to be anything but boring.

CHAPTER TEN

SEVERAL DAYS LATER, Selena shivered as she stared into the eyes of three men long dead.

This was something she hadn't bargained for when she'd taken on the mural project. She'd opted to start adding color to the center panel of the fire station mural first, maybe subconsciously hoping to get the worst part over with. Maybe she'd known it would shake her up.

Adding details to the firefighters' eyes had done it. She supposed it was a sign that she'd gotten the sparkle, the life in them just right, but that was little consolation at the moment.

These heroic men had lost their lives on the job. They'd be frozen in time on this wall for years to come, always the same age. David Acevedo had died at thirty-two. Jimmy Adolf at thirty-eight. And Frank Werschler, twenty-seven. Frank, in particular, broke Selena's heart. He was her age. Younger than Evan. Hadn't ever gotten to be in his thirties. From what she'd read, he'd left behind a wife and three young children to somehow go on living without him.

Selena knew firsthand the survivors had never gone back to "normal." Knew that whatever had happened, they'd had to fill holes the size of the Grand Canyon in their lives. There was no way to ignore the empty chair at the dinner table, no way to avoid the excruciating finality of sorting through the belongings of a loved one.

For her, the aftermath of losing her father, even though he'd been FBI and not a firefighter, had meant the breaking apart of her family. Her mother had changed after that. In one fell swoop, Selena had, in essence, lost both of her parents. She wondered how deep the deaths of these men had rocked their own families' foundations. Couldn't help thinking about the price the children and other loved ones ended up paying.

Instinctively, she placed her left hand on her abdomen as fear for her child overcame her. So many things in this life that she might not be able to shield the little one from... How did parents handle that? How did they let go of the fears and focus on the joys? Her mother certainly hadn't been able to. Why did she think *she* could do any better?

Tears blinded her as she tried to touch up Frank's chin. She ended up having to put her brush down. Sucking in heavy, humid air, she struggled to regain her composure.

Selena decided now was as good a time as any to take a break. She went to her bag and pulled out an apple, then circled around to the unpainted backside of the wall. Sitting on the pavement, she sagged against the wall, bone tired.

Part of her mood was first-trimester fatigue, she didn't doubt, but that was just a fraction of her problem. She pushed herself hard on her paintings each night, working into the early hours to get as many done as she could. She and Macey had discussed the benefits of producing more now in the hope of being able to do less later. After the baby was born.

Her first works of art were currently being produced onto merchandise and would be available in some of the local gift shops within a week. She'd chosen several beach scenes for the company Macey had hooked her up with to create tote and beach bags, coasters, makeup bags and key chains. Plus she'd secured consignment space in a gallery on the island and had four originals up for sale. The high prices the gallery owner had put on her work had shocked her. But she'd tried to hide her reaction, to seem like a seasoned pro—even though before now, she'd never offered a single piece for sale.

The alarm erupted from the fire station. Her body reacted automatically, her heart racing and her mouth going dry.

Evan was on duty.

She sat up straighter so she could watch the truck pull out of the bay. In less than two minutes, the bright red front appeared and it pulled into the street.

There he was. Backseat, passenger side.

Please let this call be no big deal. A false alarm, even.

Scenes flashed through her mind of burning buildings, choking smoke. Probably from TV shows, and her imagination had only been stoked by her own recent fire.

As the truck sped off north, the ambulance trailing it, Selena closed her eyes and prayed for Evan's safety.

"Are you sleeping on the job?"

Selena sprang to attention and opened her eyes, relieved to see it was only Macey walking toward her from the main door of the station.

"How are you so calm?" Selena asked her.

"Why wouldn't I be? Just took lunch to Derek."

Macey stared at Selena, whose eyes had strayed back to the empty bay. Macey glanced that way. "Oh, the call? Did that upset you?"

"I shouldn't worry. I barely know him, whereas you're engaged. Derek was driving."

Macey smiled. "Such a boy. He loves driving the truck."

Selena studied her, searching for some sign of panic. "How do you do it?"

"Do what?"

"How do you watch them drive off toward danger without losing your mind?"

Macey stared up the street where the truck had disappeared and shrugged. "Big fires are rare. The really dangerous stuff doesn't happen every day."

"But there's risk every single time they go out," Selena said.

"Sure. There's risk every time one of us gets into a car." Macey slid her back down the wall and sat next to Selena, who had slumped back down.

"Different odds. Are you really able to *not* worry when he's at work?"

"I can't. If I did, I'd be a head case and need a padded white room."

"You just…don't? How?"

"Self-preservation. And I trust Derek's abilities. He wants to come home."

A different siren wailed in the distance and Selena straightened, on alert again.

"Police," Macey said. "Selena, you have to relax. You need to stay calm for the baby's sake."

"I would if I could." She put her hand on her chest

and felt her racing heart. "This is why I could never marry Evan."

Macey's head whipped toward Selena. "It sounds like you've considered it."

"For about twenty seconds. It wouldn't work, though. I couldn't live with the panic I'd feel every day he goes off to work."

Macey opened her purse and dug through it until she found a package of gum. She offered it to Selena, who'd only managed to take one bite of her apple.

"No, thanks," Selena said, distracted.

Macey unwrapped a piece and stuck it in her mouth. "Let me ask you something."

"You can ask…" Selena had noticed something in Macey's tone that worried her, told her she wasn't going to like the question at all.

"What if Evan quit his job tomorrow and became a…hmm. A construction worker. Would you marry him then?"

"Construction? You think he'd be happy with that?"

"That's not the point. For now, we'll say yes, he's incredibly excited about getting into construction. He does it by choice." Macey pegged her with a stare. "Would you?"

Selena allowed herself to imagine the scenario for a minute. "Not a fair question," she finally said.

"Ha! That tells me lots." Macey raised her chin smugly.

"The answer is I can't tell. I don't know him well enough to consider marrying him. This is all so bizarre, the situation we're in. Some people sleep around all the

time and never get 'caught.' I do it one time and wind
up pregnant."

"Shows that odds don't mean a whole lot."

"I like Evan. He's caring and giving," she said, thinking of his insistence to pay for her doctor's appointment.
"He can be bossy and stubborn."

"Can't they all. Could you ever love him? If he wasn't
a firefighter…"

"Maybe." She tried hard not to mull over the possibility most of the time.

"Are you attracted to him?"

Selena laughed. "What do you think?"

"I think he's very good-looking and has that irresist-
ible charm."

"And yet you resisted him."

"I was too busy chasing Derek."

Selena nodded. "I'm attracted to him. *Attraction* got
me into this predicament. But lust doesn't mean love,
and a marriage can't work without love. So there's your
answer."

"Lust can be the beginning of love, though. You and
Evan make such a good couple."

"Based on what?"

"I just sense it."

"Are you spouting woo-woo stuff to me?" Selena
grinned. "You want us to be together is all."

"It'd make things easier for both of you. Admit it."

"There's nothing easy about me and Evan. It's been
a twisted mess from the first night we were together."
Selena stood and brushed off her backside. "Besides…
even if I loved him, it wouldn't change that he's a firefighter. I can't handle that."

"You could work through it. If you wanted to."

"I don't. I'm trying to stay away from him as much as I can. We'll both be better off that way."

"So now would probably be a bad time to ask you to come with me to the annual fire department versus police department volleyball game?"

"Yes."

"Yes?" Macey repeated. "You'll go?"

"Yes it's a bad time to ask. When is it?" Selena asked without any enthusiasm.

"Next weekend. They make it a whole event. Put the truck out for kids to see, serve hot dogs and burgers. But the main attraction is the game. It's supposed to be entertaining—apparently they play for blood."

"Nothing I like better than watching grown men act like Neanderthals."

"Stop," Macey said, laughing. "I don't believe for a minute that you're such a killjoy. Were you like this in Boston?"

In Boston, she'd led a whirlwind social life, except for the months she'd spent caring for her brother. "No. Pregnancy tends to change a person, though."

"True. But you still need some fun. And I need someone to go to the game with. Please?"

There couldn't be too much harm in going, at least if Evan would be involved in a volleyball game. Besides, she longed to get out "with the girls," even if there was only one girl and she'd only known her for a short time.

"I'll go. But I intend to avoid Evan as much as possible, so don't get your hopes up."

"He might have something to say about that. He seems to want to be involved with the baby…and you."

"He's doing it out of duty."

"You can't be sure of that."

"Let's face it—he's an honorable guy," Selena said. "Honorable guys don't shirk their responsibilities. I just need to make it crystal clear that he is *not* responsible for me or this child and that we are *not* his duty."

"Good luck with that," Macey said, also standing. "I think you're kidding yourself if you believe he'll walk away."

"He can't force me to marry him."

"But he can force you to give him access to his child. What are you going to do about that?"

"No idea yet. I was hoping he'd get over this insistence to be involved."

"Those guys, the firefighters, most of them are like that. Very conscious of their duty."

"That's what I'm afraid of," Selena muttered.

She walked back around to the mural and picked up her brush. This was going to be a long fight, but she wasn't going to back down.

CHAPTER ELEVEN

EVAN WAS DOING his best to worm his way into Selena's life.

In the past week, since she'd made the mistake of kissing him, he'd called to check on her several times, brought her a supply of soda crackers and tried to take her out. She'd refused, using work as a somewhat legitimate excuse. The only thing she'd succumbed to was the doctor's appointment, and of course he'd insisted on coming with her. There'd been no way to say no, not when he was paying for it.

Now, as she sat on the exam table in the office of a doctor recommended by Evan's acquaintances, reality was bearing down on her in a way it hadn't before.

Sure, she'd acknowledged her life was going to change drastically. Had considered what the pregnancy would do to her body. Had even allowed herself to envision a sweet, cooing baby in her life. But it'd been a distant, vague concept.

Looking around at the small room, there was no way to keep things vague or distant in her mind anymore.

Posters lined the walls of the otherwise warmly decorated room: monthly fetal development, changes in the pregnant woman's body, baby growth charts. The magazine selection was a dichotomy of hardcore sports and parenting/pregnancy. Swollen bellies flashed at her from every surface. And that didn't even include the wall of pamphlets on a multitude of pregnancy and newborn topics including some she never would've imagined in a hundred years.

A quick knock signaled the nurse's arrival and forced Selena's attention from one fear to another.

"Good morning," the blonde nurse said. She was close to Selena's age and tiny—barely five feet tall, if that. Her cute, freckled face was full of warmth and Selena clung to that.

"Hi."

"Your first pregnancy?" the nurse—Kelsy, according to her name tag—asked.

Selena nodded, unsure her voice would work.

The nurse perused the forms Selena had filled out in the lobby, asking questions as she went along.

"Is Dad here today?" Kelsy asked, and it took Selena a few seconds to realize who she referred to. Dad. The father. Evan.

Duh.

"He's in the waiting room," she finally explained, plastering a smile on her face in hopes of hiding that this wasn't a happy family in the making.

"Dr. Martin usually likes to check things out with an ultrasound the first appointment, as long as you're far enough along. Sound okay?"

Selena nodded. There was no doubt in her mind about when the baby was conceived. She told the nurse the date of conception and Kelsy entered the information on her laptop.

"We should be able to see the fetal heart beating. Would you like Dad to join us?"

Hearing Evan referred to as Dad weirded Selena out.

He wasn't Dad—he was the hot guy who'd gotten her mind off her family problems for an evening. And a night and part of a morning if you wanted to get technical.

"Uh, sure," Selena said, not sure about any of it and wondering if she could back things up by about two months and get a do-over.

"What's his name? I'll call him in once we get you settled in the ultrasound room."

"Evan."

He was going to love this. Not.

Selena followed the nurse to the end of the hallway and into a larger room with a handy supply of scary-looking equipment.

"Undress from the waist down. There's a sheet on the bed to drape over your legs. Lie on your back on the table and relax. We'll give you time to undress and then they'll be in."

Kelsy disappeared before Selena could process what was about to happen. She couldn't think of anything worse than getting naked at the doctor's office—except getting naked and then having a man she barely knew in the exam room with her.

She hurried to the door and whipped it open, frantic to stop the nurse. But there was no one in the hall. She shut the door in a panic.

Okay. Plan B. Kelsy would be showing Evan in any second and if Selena was still dressed and freaked-out, it'd be obvious this guy wasn't the love of her life. Easy to figure out Selena had screwed up royally and was on the path to single parenthood. Best to undress and cover as thoroughly and securely as possible with the paper-thin gown. Fast. Because if she didn't move now, she'd be standing in the middle of the room half-naked when Evan walked in, and that, too, would be mortifying.

She unsnapped her jeans and yanked them down her legs, nearly tripping over them. Folding them sloppily, she tossed them on one of the chairs. She sucked in a breath for courage, then took her panties off, sticking them under her jeans. With a glance at the door, she grabbed the sheet and wrapped it securely around her waist.

By the time the door squeaked open, she was on her back, hopefully well covered, her eyes closed.

"Hey," Evan said as casually as if she was sitting there snacking on a bag of chips.

Selena opened her eyes and was relieved he was alone.

"Sorry to make you come in here. I didn't realize what I was getting myself into. You don't have to stay if you don't want to."

He took her hand—the one that wasn't holding her flowy, ruffly shirt down over the top of the sheet as if national security depended on it—and squeezed it gently.

"You look worried," he said quietly.

"I'm not a big fan of being half-naked at the doctor's office. On the exam table, no less."

He smiled. "It's better than completely naked. They said we're going to see the baby's heartbeat?"

"I guess so. Believe me, I'm as clueless about this as you. And I was serious that you don't have to stay."

"I'd like to. It's not every day a guy can see a microscopic heart beating on a screen. Especially one that he helped create."

She looked closely at him, searching for humor or

sarcasm, but as far as she could tell, he was genuinely excited. Of course, he wasn't the one who had to have instruments stuck God knew where.

"Hello," a woman's voice called out before the door opened all the way. "All ready?"

Selena nodded, and Evan said, "Come in."

"I'm Dr. Martin," the brunette in her late thirties said, holding her hand out to shake theirs.

She made small talk and went over some of the basic information about the pregnancy just as the nurse had done. She did a quick exam, then began explaining how the internal ultrasound would work. She claimed it wouldn't hurt, but Selena never trusted any medical personnel who said that.

"Ease up, darlin'," Evan said quietly into her ear.

When Selena turned to question him, he was leaning down and his head was right next to hers, close enough for her to feel his breath.

"You're cutting off the circulation in my hand," he said. "It's okay."

She exhaled and loosened her grip.

"Are we ready?" the doctor asked.

Selena wanted to clarify that "we" was a misleading word since it was really her who would be on the receiving end of the torture, but instead she bit her tongue and nodded, scared out of her mind. She squeezed her eyes shut.

By the time Evan convinced her to open them, the overhead light had been turned out and the wand was undoubtedly doing what the wand was supposed to do in parts that she really wished were left private. It wasn't as uncomfortable as Selena had feared—and then she forgot all about the wand completely.

"There it is," Dr. Martin said.

She dared to peek at the screen, following the doctor's pointer to a small blip that pulsed regularly.

"That's your baby's heart," the doctor said. "Pounding away strongly." She pointed out very general body areas of the fetus and Selena finally made out the shape of the alien being in her womb.

Except it wasn't an alien. It was a baby. Fetus. Whatever. A little living being that would soon grow into a big living being that would require care day and night.

Nausea welled in Selena's gut and she couldn't seem to get enough oxygen. She closed her eyes again, trying to block out the sight and sucking in air as if it was in short supply.

"Selena?" Evan caressed her hand and leaned over her. "What's wrong?"

She shook her head, still breathing deeply and fighting the terror that seeped into her every cell. Finally, the wand went away and the overhead light came back on. Selena kept her eyes shut while the doctor washed her hands and rolled the machinery to the side of the room again.

"Everything looks great so far," Dr. Martin said. "The size is right where it should be. Based on the date of conception the baby's due date is June twenty-eighth." She sat on her stool and rolled closer to the exam table. "Is everything okay, sweetie?"

Selena forced her eyes open and nodded.

"Do either of you have any questions for me?"

"Is there anything Selena shouldn't do?" Evan asked.

Selena couldn't have come up with a coherent question if someone paid her, and considering she had to pay a deductible on her insurance claim on the house, that was saying a lot. Her chest had constricted and hurt right in the center. There still didn't seem to be enough oxygen in the room, and closing her eyes really did nothing to stop the way her body felt. She wondered briefly if she was having a heart attack and figured if she was, this was the place to do it.

The doctor was going on to Evan about something—Selena tuned in just in time to hear her final sentence.

"The two of you can have a normal sex life and continue to have intercourse for as long as it's comfortable."

At that, Selena sat up and leaned forward, hands over her face, ready to cover her parts and escape.

"Good to know," Evan replied to the doctor, and Selena could hear the smile in his voice. "Thanks, Doctor. We'll see you in about a month."

The doctor congratulated them and left them alone. Selena climbed down from the torture bed and hurried to the chair to retrieve her clothes. Keeping the sheet wrapped around her like a skirt, she pulled her panties on, her back to Evan. She finally let the sheet drop, sat on the chair, and jammed both her legs into her jeans at once.

"Are you okay?" Evan asked, bending down in front of her. His voice was gentle. That made tears well up in her eyes and all she could do was shake her head.

She was so not okay.

"I have to get out of here."

CHAPTER TWELVE

AT THE RECEPTION DESK, Evan tapped the pen on the counter as he waited for the slip to sign. Selena had run out of the doctor's office as though she had a swarm of killer bees after her. He'd be surprised if she was waiting in his truck. Something was definitely wrong. She didn't show any of the awe he'd expected—hell, that he'd felt himself—at the sight of the tiny beating heart. Sure, the pregnancy wasn't planned, and they were both trying to adjust to the news, but seeing that pulse on the monitor was a big deal.

"Would you like to set up the next appointment now?" the receptionist asked as she finally handed over the receipt. The ultrasound made it an expensive afternoon, but he was serious about getting her the best care available. He'd gladly pay extra for that.

"I'll have her call," Evan said. He had no idea where the two of them would be in four weeks, but *stable* wasn't a word he'd use to describe their situation. At the rate they were going, it would take longer than four weeks to convince her to marry him. "Thank you."

He hurried out the door of the office into what had become a gray, overcast day. Selena wasn't in the truck. Big shock. But where the hell was she?

A glance up and down the sidewalk told him she wasn't hoofing it back home. Finally, he spotted her sitting against the base of a palm tree at the side of the building, facing away from him.

He walked slowly toward her, unsure of what he was supposed to do or say. He needed to tread lightly.

When he got to the tree, he slid down the trunk on the opposite side from her. As he landed on the river rocks that lined the plant bed, he grimaced.

"What's going on, Selena?"

She didn't speak. As they sat there for what felt like aeons, the wind picked up, rustling through the trees, and large raindrops began to fall. Evan was on the verge of suggesting they relocate to the truck when Selena spoke up.

"I can't have a baby."

A drop nailed him in the cheek and he wiped away the moisture. "Okay. Why not?"

Something landed on the rocks in front of her and he guessed she'd thrown one of the fist-size stones.

"I don't know how to be a mom."

"Does anybody?"

"I've never even held a baby, Evan. I worked with kids, but they were all older. Walking. Talking."

He'd been in a similar situation when his twin sister, Melanie, had had a baby a few months ago. "You'll hold ours and some kind of motherly instinct will kick in out of nowhere. I'm sure of it. Saw it happen with my sister."

She shook her head almost frantically. "Instincts don't matter. You can still screw it up."

The drops started coming faster and Evan hopped up. He went around to her and held out his hand. "Let's continue this in the truck."

She gazed up at him stubbornly and he thought for

sure she was going to refuse. At last, she stood—surprising him by taking his hand.

He followed her to the passenger side and opened the door for her. He jogged around to his side and got in just as the clouds opened up.

Now what did he say? There was nothing in his life that had prepared him for this situation.

"You could call a friend back home. Family member. Do you have a sister?"

Selena shook her head distractedly.

"You can't talk to your mom?"

Selena laughed hollowly. "No, I can't talk to my mom. She's in the screwing-it-up category. I haven't talked to her for over a month now."

"Don't suppose you're going to tell me what happened with her." He watched her for a reaction but got nothing. "Did you two fight?"

"For fifteen years, give or take."

"Did you leave home because of her?"

"You could say that."

They sat there with the rain pelting down on the cab of the truck and the wind whipping the palm fronds outside the window. Their breath had fogged up the glass so that the world was a blur, but then life seemed like a blur lately, so maybe this was fitting.

"I told my mom and brother I don't want them in my life anymore. Don't want to be in theirs," Selena said, so quietly he could barely hear her over the storm. "I couldn't take it anymore so I packed up my stuff and left."

"And came here? From Boston?"

"I didn't know where else to go. My friends idolize

my brother and like my mother. They don't get how I feel."

"What made you decide on San Amaro Island?"

"I came here when I was a little girl," she said. "Remembered it as a peaceful place, full of good memories. I thought it would make me feel better."

"Does it?"

She shook her head. "Makes me realize how alone I am."

"What did you and your mom argue about?"

Selena turned as if just now realizing who she was talking to. "You don't want to hear all this. I'm sorry."

"I asked."

She drew her left leg toward her and leaned against the door. "My brother, Tom, is in the army. Special Forces. Just over a year ago, he was in an explosion and almost died." Her voice broke on the last words and she wouldn't make eye contact.

Jeez. "That's rough," he said.

"I took care of him once he was able to come home. It was basically a full-time job at first, monitoring his medications, surgeries, therapy sessions, helping him eat. I'd been volunteering five days a week at the Art to Heart Center and I stopped going so that I could help him get his life back."

"That's a big sacrifice."

"Nothing compared to what he went through." She rubbed her upper arms and Evan reached into the backseat to grab the sweatshirt he'd left there. He handed it to her and she slipped it over her head. "Thanks. It took ten months for my brother to recover. He was one of the lucky ones. He lost two men in the explosion and another three were crippled by the blast."

"I'm glad he's okay," Evan said, watching her. She didn't offer more. "So how did you go from being his caretaker to leaving him?"

"He's back in Iraq, Afghanistan, who knows where exactly," she said quietly, as if that explained everything.

"Takes some *cajones,* I'll give him that."

"Takes a bunch of rocks for a brain!" Selena fisted her hands in her lap. "After almost dying, he chose to go back there. To put himself in that danger again. I understand the whole serve-your-country thing—to an extent. Understand that the military is something he had to do. But he *almost died.* We almost *lost* him. And he went back to it willingly." Barely controlled rage laced her words.

As someone who thrived on facing unknown dangers every day in his job—granted, different kinds of dangers from having a mine go off in his face, but still dangers—Evan could understand her brother's decision. His job was so much a part of him that if he stopped doing it, his life wouldn't be quite right.

He doubted mentioning that he understood where her brother was coming from would score any points with Selena right now, though.

"How does your mom fit into it?"

A growl of frustration came from Selena's throat. "She's big on her social life, big on appearances. When my brother announced he was going back, do you know what that woman did? She used it as an excuse to throw a party! 'Hey, let's celebrate! My son's going back to see if the bad guys can do him in completely this time. What a great chance to show I can host the party of the year!'"

Evan put a hand on Selena's thigh, wanting to calm her down before she went through the ceiling. He didn't speak, though…had no idea which words would be the right ones.

"I left town on the day of the party. Drove for three days to get here. The night I met you is the day my brother left for duty."

Everything clicked into place. Her recklessness, her openness to going home with him, the one-eighty in personality she'd pulled since. She'd been scared of losing a member of her family, and had blown off some serious steam—with him.

"Have you talked to your mom or brother since you left?"

"What do you think?"

"I think you're an expert at call avoidance," he said with a half grin. "I'm going to vote no."

"I had one of my friends tell my mom I'm safe, so she doesn't try to track me down. I don't want to talk to her. Don't want either one of them in my life. I'm much better off by myself than having to wait for a phone call saying my brother is dead."

"Which brings us back to you needing someone to talk to."

"I don't need someone to talk to. I just need…I don't know. Ice cream."

Evan chuckled, relieved to see evidence of her sense of humor. She didn't look quite as pale, either. He checked his watch and started the truck.

"Where are we going?" Selena asked as she buckled her seat belt.

"Lambert's opens at ten."

"You don't have to—"

"You're getting ice cream. No arguments."

"I'm going to weigh five hundred pounds."

"Start thinking about what flavor you want."

Ten minutes later, Evan returned to the truck, where Selena waited, with a large drink for himself, a butter pecan sundae for her and a plan of action for the rest of the day.

"Buckle up, darlin'. We've got somewhere to go."

"Home?" Selena asked as she straightened from her slouch and took the big foam dish from him.

"You can't work on the mural in the rain, correct?"

"Right, but I can work in my studio."

"Light's horrible. Besides, you have plans." He started the engine and backed out of the parking spot.

"What are my plans?" she asked warily.

"A surprise."

He glanced over at her in time to see her narrow her eyes.

"Trust me," he said, knowing she had no reason to. But then she really had no reason not to, either.

"How long will this surprise take?"

"All day. What do you have to lose?"

"A day. I really should be painting."

"It'll wait. You need a mental health day."

She eyed him sideways. "I'm not sure I like what you're insinuating."

Evan smiled. "You are difficult."

"Because I won't bend to your will and go who knows where with you for the whole day? Or because I won't marry you?"

"Yes."

"Why should I go?"

"Because it might, in some small way, be helpful. You might even have fun."

"What is this word, 'fun'?"

Evan grinned. "Last chance. Here's where I get on the highway and take you away. Unless you stop me."

Selena looked at the road and back at him. "Go ahead. Have your way with me."

She said it with more dread than humor, but Evan couldn't help the thoughts that flooded his mind about how he would like to have his way with her again. He didn't kid himself. While marriage hadn't been in his plans, there would definitely be some perks of sharing a bed with Selena every night.

CHAPTER THIRTEEN

ALL SELENA HAD PRIED out of Evan on the nearly two-hour car trip was that they were going to drop by his twin sister's house and that his sister and her husband had a three-month-old son. Contrary to what Evan apparently thought, this served to do nothing but inspire terror in Selena.

First off, there had been no discussion of meeting each other's families. That wasn't even on her radar and now she was minutes away from it.

Help me, God.

Not only family, but a baby, too. A baby was helpless and fragile and scared the living daylights out of her. What if she did something wrong? What if she somehow scarred him for life? She had plenty of experience with baby dolls but none with the real, squirming, breathing thing.

The truck's turn signal clicked as they approached an exit, and Selena's body shifted into overdrive—heart rate up, blood pressure up, stress up. Maybe she would throw up while she was at it.

"Try to relax," Evan said. "I think you'll like Melanie."

She doubted she would like anything in the next few hours, but what could she do? With a deep breath, she put on an everything's-fine mask and forced a smile for Evan.

He pulled into the driveway of a house the size of a glorified shoe box, and yet Selena was immediately struck by the homeyness it. It was painted light blue and had a flower box beneath each of two symmetrical windows on the front facade. There were three steps up to the door, and the concrete was lined with pots of plants.

"Ready?" Evan asked as he cut the engine.

"Not in the least. Evan, this was never part of the deal."

"What? Meeting my sister? She's just my sister. A twenty-nine-year-old new mom who would love to meet you."

"Let's get it over with."

"Try to tone down your enthusiasm. Don't want to come on too strong to her or the baby."

Selena climbed out of the truck before Evan could get to her side. She wasn't in the mood for him to be nice to her.

He knocked softly on the front door, and it swung open seconds later.

"You made it," his sister said, stepping outside and throwing her arms around Evan.

She had strawberry-blond hair and was tall and mostly slender except for a bit of a postbaby stomach and shockingly large breasts. Freckles were sprinkled across her cheeks and nose. She spotted Selena over Evan's shoulder.

"Hello. You must be Selena. I'm Melanie."

Selena awkwardly offered a hand for her to shake and nodded. "Nice to meet you."

"Evan said he was bringing you along, but he was very mysterious."

"He's like that," Selena said, eyeing him sideways.

"Where's the little man?" Evan asked, opening the door wider.

"Napping," Melanie said in a hushed voice. She led them into the living room.

As Melanie motioned for them to sit, they heard baby gurgles coming from the next room.

"Or not. Be right back, y'all." Melanie left and Evan moved closer to Selena as she glanced around. The inside was as inviting as the outside of the house. Curtains she'd noticed from the driveway had a delicate flower print and matching ribbons holding them back. Coordinated throw pillows covered the chairs, and an afghan was draped over the back of the sofa. A small bookshelf in the corner overflowed with books, and framed photos lined the top shelf. A delicious, sweet aroma wafted in from the kitchen.

"Cute house," Selena said to Evan, walking to the shelf of photos to see if she could spot him in any. It didn't take long—he was in Melanie's wedding picture, as well as several others.

"She's Holly Homemaker to an extreme," Evan said, and Selena didn't miss the affection in his voice.

Melanie returned with a tiny baby cradled in her arms. She was playing with his nose and he flashed a toothless grin every time she touched him.

"This is Henry," Melanie said, totally absorbed in her son, and honestly, Selena could kind of see why. He was absolutely adorable and the way he grinned and responded to his mom…it made something deep inside her go warm and soft.

"Henry, my main man, come here to Uncle Evan."

Melanie handed him over and Evan held him against his chest.

Selena's insides went from warm to completely puddled at the sight of this big man clearly head over heels with the baby. His hands looked huge as they supported Henry's head, and yet he was so gentle.

Gah. She was becoming a hopeless sap. She couldn't help imagining him loving *their* child like that, though, and, oddly, that vision brought tears to her eyes.

Idiot, Selena said to herself. *You can't have it both ways. You and he do not equal a family, so get over it.*

Evan pressed his lips to Henry's forehead and then held his nephew a few inches over his head, eliciting the biggest grin yet. "You've doubled in size, little man. Your mama must be feeding you day and night."

"If you only knew how true that was," Melanie said, and Selena noticed the shadows of fatigue under her eyes. "He's a piglet."

"You need to let your mama sleep," Evan told Henry, bringing him up so close to his face that their noses touched.

"Why don't you two entertain Henry for a couple of minutes and I'll bring out drinks and a snack."

"You don't need to go to any trouble," Selena said, thinking how overwhelming it must be to take care of an infant all day every day…and night.

"No trouble at all. I made chocolate-chip cookies when Evan called to say you were coming."

"You baked cookies? With a newborn? I'm impressed," Selena said.

"I cheated. They're slice and bake. But they do in a pinch."

"I told you she's the domestic goddess," Evan said. "It's best to do what she says and eat some cookies."

"Is tea okay?" Melanie asked.

"Does it have caffeine?" Evan asked, surprising Selena.

"Not a drop. I'm trying to stay away from it while I'm nursing."

"Sounds good," Selena said, wondering if Evan had told her why they were visiting when he called her earlier.

Melanie disappeared to the kitchen and Evan lowered himself to the sofa. Selena sat next to him, unable to take her eyes off Henry.

"He's so cute," she said.

"Of course he is. My mom says he looks like I used to."

"Your modesty is impressive."

"Want to hold him?"

"No." She stared at Henry's doll-like facial features, completely enchanted by him and yet uneasy.

"You weren't kidding about not being comfortable around babies."

Selena shook her head. None of her friends had children yet. Only a couple from her circle were even married. She didn't have any babies in her family. Hers would be the first.

"I hadn't, either," Evan admitted. "Not till this guy." He made a face at Henry and earned a gurgle.

"You seem to know what you're doing."

"Nah. If he needs anything, I hand him over to Mel."

Selena continued to watch Henry. He put his itty-bitty

hand in his mouth and sucked on his knuckles for all he was worth. His other hand flailed toward Selena's side. Without thinking, she stuck her index finger out to touch him. Before she knew it, he'd grasped her finger and held on.

"Kid's got some good taste," Evan said. "Sure you don't want to try holding him? I'll be right next to you."

Henry's big blue eyes were focused on her now and she was mesmerized. "Okay. Come here, Henry."

Evan helped her settle Henry on her legs, his head near her knees. The baby returned his gaze to Selena. His arms were extended and constantly in motion and Selena stuck out her pinky finger and let him grip it.

Eyes wide, Henry put his other hand in his mouth again.

Selena watched him intently, fascinated by his every jerky movement. She barely noticed when Melanie returned and set down tall glasses of sweet tea on coasters on the coffee table.

Henry noticed, though, and peered toward his mom.

"Hey, little boy, who's got you?" Melanie asked. She sat in one of the two armchairs across from the sofa, her attention riveted on her son.

Suddenly the sweet, smooth baby face wrinkled into a frown, and then he let out a full-size wail. Selena tensed and looked frantically at Melanie.

"Your mama's still here, little man," Evan said. "Right over there. You inherited her lungs, didn't you?"

"I upset him," Selena said, begging Melanie with her eyes to take him back.

"Not at all," Melanie said, standing and picking up

a baby cloth from the end and coming toward her son. "He just woke up and wants to nurse."

"I can't help you there," Selena said, putting her hand under Henry's neck as she'd seen Evan do and lifting him.

"Come here," Melanie said, bending down and taking the baby. She sat back in her chair, then started talking about their mother to Evan as she lifted her T-shirt, unlatched something on her bra and let the baby begin drinking, just like that. Selena looked away. She'd never seen an infant nurse up close and was surprised at the pull on her emotions. She tried to imagine feeding her own child but couldn't wrap her brain around it.

"So, Selena, Evan told me on the phone that you're expecting. When's the due date?"

"Um, end of June." Selena glanced up at Evan, wondering what else he'd told his sister. "The twenty-eighth."

"A summer baby. You'll be ready to have it by then."

"I don't know. The pregnancy...wasn't planned. I'm not feeling ready for anything at all."

"Mel," Evan said, his tone serious. "There's something I didn't tell you on the phone. The baby's mine."

Melanie's eyes widened and then she squealed. "Omigod, Evan! How could you keep that to yourself?"

"As Selena said, it wasn't planned. Not quite the same as you and Brad."

Melanie looked from Evan to Selena and back. "Okay. Then I guess congratulations is the wrong thing to say?"

"We're still figuring things out," Evan said.

Selena held her breath, waiting for him to mention his marriage campaign, dreading pressure from his sister. But he didn't bring it up.

"I have a couple of pregnancy books you can borrow," Melanie said to Selena. "They helped a ton. Believe me, it's scary even when you plan it and pray for it."

"Thank you," Selena said, overcome by this woman's kindness. "Scary is an understatement. Henry is the first baby I've held."

"Aw, Henry, did you hear that?"

He didn't stir—intent as he was on nursing.

"You're going to have a cousin," Melanie said to her son.

The words made Selena squirm. She hadn't begun to consider telling anyone in her family about her pregnancy, let alone think about Evan's relatives and whether or not they would be involved. It was all too complex and hard to swallow.

"I'd appreciate it if you don't mention anything to Mom yet," Evan told his sister. "She needs to hear it from me."

"When are you going to tell her?"

"As soon as I convince Selena to marry me."

So much for the gratitude she'd been feeling.

"We're not getting married," she said, trying to keep the edge out of her voice.

They avoided the topic for the next few minutes. Henry finished nursing and Melanie burped him as they talked.

Henry let out a grown-up-size belch, making all three of them laugh. "That he gets from his daddy," Melanie said.

"Wonder what our kiddo will inherit from each of us," Evan said.

"Will y'all find out the baby's gender before it's born?" Melanie asked.

"I'm not sure," Selena said, wearier and more emotionally spent than she'd been in a long time. "I haven't thought about it yet."

"I want to know as soon as we can," Evan said.

"Maybe." Selena clenched her teeth. He was invading her life and her pregnancy bit by bit, slowly bowling her over and continually shocking her with the amount he wanted to be involved. She never would have guessed.

This man who insisted on being right there for every detail of her pregnancy was so in contrast with the sexy, larger-than-life charmer she'd first met at the bar. That man had been safer. She wouldn't fall for him.

She couldn't deny that in a perfect world, she'd want this Evan in her life and the child's. She'd want the family, and there could even be a chance of them being a happy one. She was obviously insanely attracted to him. He was an honorable, caring man. But his job was a deal breaker. It colored everything and made it impossible for Selena to let herself care about him. She wished he was only the sexy-surface-stranger she met in the bar.

She closed her eyes as Melanie and Evan reminisced about Melanie's pregnancy and the friendly family battle over the baby's name. Everything had been the way it should be for Melanie and her husband, it seemed. Happily married, ready to start a family. A built-in support system of parents and siblings. The way it sounded, the biggest dilemma had been whether to name the baby after a family member or give him his very own name.

Selena had screwed up royally. Not just by being irresponsible for a night. It was as if she'd gone out and picked the most heartbreaking candidate to be the father of her child—someone caring and responsible, someone who, in other circumstances, she could imagine raising a family with. Someone who, in reality, she could never let her guard down enough to fall in love with.

Pressure built behind her eyes and in her throat.

The front door opened and a man wearing green scrubs walked in.

"Hey, babe," he said to Melanie.

"Look who's here, Henry. Daddy!" Melanie stood and handed the baby to her husband, who leaned in to kiss her. "Evan brought his friend Selena here for a visit."

She made introductions, omitting the reason Selena and Evan were there. Brad reached out to shake Selena's hand after he shifted Henry to his left arm.

"Henry's the star of the show here," he said, and the sparkle of pride in his eyes, along with the way he pulled Melanie close to him, hit Selena in the gut. This was what family should be.

They sat and talked for another hour about comfortable topics: Brad's medical residency, Evan and Melanie's mother, the island and more. Evan ended up confiding about Selena's pregnancy and Brad handled it well and didn't make a big deal of it. Selena sagged back into the cushions in relief once the subject changed again.

"Did you get that boat?" Brad asked Evan.

"No, man," Evan said, and Selena caught a hint of his disappointment—before he pasted a grin on his face.

"What?" Brad and Melanie questioned him at once.

"Decided against it."

"Was there something wrong with the one you'd picked out?" Brad asked. "I thought you said it was perfect."

"It was. Bad timing is all."

Selena studied him as Brad continued to ask him about the features, price, model. Evan's face lit up as he spoke and she wondered…was the baby the reason he'd backed out? Whatever the cause, she gathered it was a hefty sacrifice for him. Yet another repercussion of their bad luck.

"We should go soon," Selena said after a while, dying to escape.

She'd held the baby, gotten a taste of how cute one could be, witnessed the painful antithesis of her near future, and now she needed to be alone. She wasn't a member of Evan's family and never wanted to be, even though she really liked his sister, brother-in-law and their baby. But it was one more connection she couldn't afford to make only to lose it.

"I thought you didn't have to work," Evan said.

"I need to finish a painting tonight. Besides, Melanie and Brad have enough to do without entertaining us."

"It's been great to have adult conversation, actually," Melanie said. "But it sounds like you have a lot to do."

"Let me say goodbye to the man," Evan said, standing and taking his nephew from Melanie's arms. "Come here, big guy." He swung him up high again, eliciting a big grin and a wad of drool. "Next time I see you I'll get you started on surf lessons."

Henry made contented baby noises as Evan drew him close and kissed his chubby cheeks. Selena's heart constricted painfully. He was so gentle with his nephew. He'd be a wonderful father.…

"I'm glad you came," Melanie said. "Evan can give you my phone number and e-mail address so you can holler if you want to talk pregnancy or baby stuff."

"Thank you," Selena said. She would definitely have a thousand questions before this was over. While Macey was well intentioned, she'd never been through pregnancy, and when Selena thought of her friends from Boston, she couldn't imagine breaking the news to them. Unwed pregnancy wasn't something they discussed. "Your son is amazing."

"Yours will be, too. Talk to you soon." She took Henry from Evan and put her arm around her brother. "Love you, Evan. Call me."

"Take care, guys," Brad said.

Selena and Evan didn't talk during the ride home.

It was too much. Watching the happy family of three tore Selena up because she wouldn't have that. This baby would be shortchanged from day one. Their child would never have what Henry did.

CHAPTER FOURTEEN

"Isn't that one of your women over there?" Clay asked Evan between serves. They were in the middle of game two of the annual fundraiser. After losing the first game by three points, the firefighters were fired up, determined to force a third against the police department.

Evan craned his neck to follow Clay's gaze into the crowd along the waterside. "It's Jenny." Not his. He didn't have a woman, but he'd immediately thought of Selena when Clay said it.

He'd gone out with Jenny twice but hadn't gotten around to calling her again. Then Selena had shown up.

Like it or not, everything had changed since Selena.

He hadn't talked to her since he'd dropped her off after their visit to Melanie's. Two days, not that he was counting. Dammit, so maybe he was.

"Not bad," Clay said, still checking Jenny out. "You going to ask her out again?"

Jorge Consuelo, the cop with the biggest mouth on the island, served the volleyball then and Evan dove for it. Clay set it near the net and Scott Pataki, one of the paramedics, spiked it. For being such a skinny dude, Pataki had some power. The ball landed just inside the line on the other team's side.

"Eat that," Scott said as a couple of the other firefighters hooted.

"Y'all are all talk. Enjoy the game, because we're gonna finish it off real quick." Jorge had a cocky grin on his face.

Evan dusted himself off and addressed Clay. "No, I'm not going to ask her out again. Why would I?"

"You sure you're not taking yourself off the market prematurely?" Derek asked from the other side of him.

"You haven't seen Selena for a few days, have you?" Clay added.

"What is with you guys?"

"I'm in favor of it if you're getting serious," Derek said. "Just want to make sure it's a two-way thing."

"Did you change her mind yet?" Clay asked.

Evan nearly snarled at both of them. "I'm giving her some space."

His idea of taking her to meet Melanie had backfired. When he'd dropped her off that evening, she'd been quiet, distant. He'd let her go without any questions. He hadn't been sure what to say, how *not* to make things worse.

He'd hoped to hear from her in the meantime, or at least have a chance to talk to her at the station when she was painting. The time he'd gone looking for her during his shift, though, she'd either been on a break or gone for the day.

Evan noticed too late that the ball was coming straight for him. He automatically held his hands out to prevent being hit in the face, but the ball bounced off his palms at the wrong angle and went out of bounds.

"Get your head in the game, Drake," Clay said. "Forget I mentioned her."

"Go to…Hades," Evan said, remembering at the last second this was a family event. Fortunately, the majority of the ankle biters were in the parking lot sitting in the driver's seat of the truck, exploring the ambulance or holding the fire hose.

There was a trophy out there and Evan didn't take to losing too well. Neither did his fellow firefighters. His reputation was on the line, and he wasn't going to endanger that because of a woman. Not today.

"FOR WANTING to avoid him, you sure haven't taken your eyes off him much," Macey said.

"I'm just watching the game," Selena lied.

"A very small part of the game." She said it with a knowing grin.

"You can't blame me for admiring from afar. It's much safer than close proximity, which I still fully plan to avoid."

"Enjoy the scenery, my friend. I know I am." Macey returned her attention to the game.

The entire team, as well as a couple of guys on the other side, had shed their shirts, even though the weather was cloudy and chilly.

Evan's tanned torso shone with sweat and his hair was a mess. The muscles on his back rippled with every movement. He stepped back and served the ball. "*That* is art," Selena said.

"Parade o' muscles." Macey made a sound of approval. "Just *look* at them."

"We're looking, honey," a woman beside them, probably close to seventy, replied. "Why else would we be here?"

"To raise money for the homeless shelter, of course," Macey said in false seriousness. "Strictly duty."

"God bless America," the woman said. "If they really want to raise some money, they ought to sell dates with those men. I'd buy a whole week. Might kill me, but I'd die one happy woman."

Before Selena could get enough of the scenery, the match was over. The firefighters had won the last two, and they celebrated their victory with high fives and chest butts. As they exited the court, they shook hands with their opponents and traded insults.

Macey dragged her through the crowd toward the court, and Selena was thankful when someone stopped them. The couple apparently knew Macey from the Shell Shack. Selena smiled politely and listened to their small talk, keeping one eye on Evan the entire time.

She caught her breath when Evan's eyes finally met hers from several feet away. He was talking to one of his colleagues, but when he spotted her, his attention became riveted to her. Selena looked away quickly.

"I'm going to find a restroom," she told Macey. "Want to meet me at the concession stand?"

Macey nodded. "I'm going to congratulate Derek first."

Before she walked off, Selena couldn't help glancing Evan's way again. He still spoke to the same person, but he'd moved slightly, so that he could keep an eye on her. She escaped, thankful for the crowd.

She'd never been such a complete, utter coward. She'd thought too much about him in the past few days, and couldn't stop dreaming about him. She was making herself nervous. And she was scared he would read her thoughts within seconds.

SELENA NEEDN'T have worried about running into Evan, it turned out. She and Macey wolfed down hot dogs at the end of a long table, while the crowd milled around them.

"Where'd Derek go?" Selena finally asked as they finished their meal.

"He had to give a short talk to the kids on fire safety. They do one every half hour or so and he gets roped in frequently. I think he actually enjoys it. He has a way with kids."

"You two thinking about babies anytime soon?" Selena asked quietly.

"I intend to make it legal first—" Macey closed her eyes. "I'm sorry. That wasn't funny like it was supposed to be."

Selena grinned. "It's okay. We can't all do it backward like me."

Macey squeezed her forearm. "I'm having my foot for dessert but what would you like?"

That made Selena laugh. "Honestly, I'm beat. I'm going to go home and take it easy for the evening."

"No working?"

"That depends. Are you asking as my business advisor or my friend?"

"Business advisor is off duty right now. And your friend says you need to relax. You deserve a night off."

"Then by all means, I must." Selena stood and bent

to hug Macey. "Thanks for making me come with you. The scenery was to die for."

"Wasn't it though. Talk to you soon. I'll be at the Shack tomorrow. Come in for lunch on me if you want to get out."

"Let's see how my painting goes. If I don't come by, I'll call you."

She waved, then found the nearest trash can to dispose of her paper plate and napkin. When she turned for home, her way was blocked by a wide, muscular chest in a San Amaro Island Fire Department T-shirt.

CHAPTER FIFTEEN

"GOING SOMEWHERE?"

Selena gathered her wits as she stared up at Evan. "Yes," she said, attempting to hide the urgency she felt. "Home."

"I'm trying not to take it personally that you didn't even say hello." He stepped closer and leaned in, giving her a sample of his fresh-showered-man scent.

"Wise of you." She lowered her gaze from his face to his chest and back again. "You're all...dressed." The image of him shirtless and muscled on the volleyball court sent heat through her veins.

"Disappointed?"

"Maybe."

"I can take my shirt off again if it would please you, miss."

Selena laughed. "I don't think so."

"You don't think it would please you?"

"I don't think it's a good idea," she clarified. "The women would flock, your ego would inflate even more..."

"The only one I care to impress is right in front of me. Unfortunately, she seems to be the one who couldn't care less."

"Good game today," Selena said quickly.

"Pulled it off in the end. I imagine we'd hear about it all year if we'd lost."

"I'm betting you'll dish it out just as much."

"You're betting right. Did you drive?"

"Macey did."

"Where's Macey?"

"Not ready to go yet."

"Which means, let me guess, you're walking. Not going to ask me for a ride?"

Selena shook her head. "Not going to ask you for a ride. But if you offered one, I'd probably accept."

"Come on."

He led her around the station to the parking lot. The sun had started to fall and the clouds had darkened. The festivities would end soon and cars were starting to file out of the lot. The main street was jammed. She was going to have to spend aeons with him alone, in his too-small cab.

Evan held Selena's hand as she climbed up. She thanked him once she was settled, her hand warm and tingly from his touch. He held her longer than necessary, and she could see raw desire in his eyes.

The kicker was that she wasn't immune to him, no matter how hard she tried to be. No matter how scared she was of getting attached. She could work herself up to a good panic attack in the middle of the night, alone in the dark when she lay there thinking about Evan in danger. But when she was this close to him, with her hand enveloped in his, it was tough to overrule what her body wanted. Watching him half-naked on the volleyball court all afternoon didn't help matters, either. It was like slow, torturous foreplay.

He walked slowly around the front of the truck and Selena tracked his every move.

"Going to storm," he said as he got in.

The palms on the edge of the parking lot swayed. "A good night to hole up and stay inside."

Their eyes met and there was no doubt in her mind what he'd like to do with the night.

She was torn. At the moment she wanted the same thing he did—for tonight. But she couldn't help being concerned about what tomorrow would bring. Could she get any closer to him, physically or otherwise, and not become tied up emotionally?

"Have you been here during a hurricane?" she asked in an attempt to get her mind off her immediate dilemma.

"Several times. Only one hit directly, a couple years ago. You don't want to be here even for the near-misses, though. Unreal, like nothing you can imagine."

"Does the fire department evacuate or do they make you stay?" Yet another concern for his safety that she hadn't considered.

"Usually we evacuate, too, but we do it as late as possible. The last time one came through, though, the storm veered off the predicted course and there was no time to get out. The island hadn't been evacuated. We had tourists everywhere." Raindrops began spattering the windshield. "I wouldn't care to go through anything like that again."

"Coming from a man who runs into fires, that's saying a lot."

"Fires, I know how to handle. They're unpredictable, but we're trained to deal with that. That storm…" He shook his head and didn't finish the thought.

"I can't imagine. First hurricane watch and I'm out of here, camped out on the mainland somewhere. Way inland."

"Smart." He smiled at her.

They were at the house before she was ready, because now she had a decision to make. She watched his profile as he pulled up and stopped. He didn't turn off the engine. It was a point in his favor that he didn't take for granted that he was welcome inside.

Lightning flashed, and a few seconds later, thunder crashed in the distance. Selena looked at the beach house, so dark and quiet and…lonely.

"Would you like to come in?" she asked.

"You're asking me inside?"

"Maybe I'm afraid of storms."

"Storms can be stressful," Evan said, his voice hushed.

"Terribly."

"Stress is bad for pregnant ladies."

"It is." She knew she was heading for trouble and attempted to backpedal. "We could talk. Watch TV. Play a rousing hand of Go Fish."

He studied her. "We could do that."

The rain came down harder, pelting the truck.

"Let's make a run for it," she said, then opened her door and slid out. She ran to the front of the house and dug out her keys, the overhang providing some protection from the downpour.

Evan came up beside her and held out his hand for the keys. Without hesitation, she gave them to him and he had the door open quickly, even though she'd forgotten to turn the porch light on. The sun had set quickly and dusk was falling, casting eerie shadows.

Evan walked in ahead of her, their fingers inter-twined. A bright streak of lightning lit up the kitchen momentarily, and before the dark returned, a deafening clap of thunder crashed, making her jump out of her skin and cling to Evan's back.

"See?" Selena said. "You thought I was kidding about storms."

"That was too close. Something got hit."

Selena let go of him and felt her way to the light switch. When she flicked it, however, nothing happened. "Something got hit, all right."

Evan headed through the dark to the newly replaced door on the beach side. He slid the glass open.

"What are you doing?" Selena asked, catching up with him.

"Just going to see if I can spot anything, figure out what got zapped."

"You're not on duty, you know."

He chuckled. "Force of habit. There could be a fire."

"Could be." She came up behind him and slipped her hands under his shirt. She ran her fingers up his back, marveling at the solid muscles that had mesmerized her during the volleyball game. She didn't stop to consider what she was doing, just let her hands go, let her senses lead her on.

"Or I could stay inside," he said quietly, turning to face her.

"You could."

His mouth came down on hers as she explored the ripples and ridges of his chest. He slid his rough hands over the sensitive skin at her waist and pulled her closer, their tongues swirling.

Just like that, she felt the fire inside her ignite, the same way it had their first night together. She'd never experienced anything like it before she'd met him, and she could finally understand how people in lust did such out-of-character things.

Evan's hands moved to her rear and he lifted her. She wrapped her legs around him, pressing herself into him, her body aching for his.

"This is crazy," she said between kisses, as she rolled his shirt up over that beautiful chest. He carried her to the wall and pressed her lightly against it with his chest, so that he could raise his arms and let her remove his shirt completely.

"It's a good crazy," he said, his voice husky and sexy enough to make her moan her agreement. That and the things he was doing with his tongue.

Thunder rolled and crashed, but Selena was barely aware of it. She was too deeply lost in Evan's kisses, his caresses, the magnificent feel of his solid body up against hers.

"Would you mind terribly," he said, "if we didn't make it to the bedroom?"

"I wouldn't mind if we ended up on the moon."

He made quick work of her shirt and tossed it on the floor. He unhooked her bra so easily she couldn't help thinking he was an expert, but when he took her breast into his mouth, all thoughts slipped out of her head.

Evan carried her to the sofa and sat down with her straddling him. Selena reveled in the heat of his chest directly on her skin. He drove her need to an excruciating height as he lavished attention on each breast, with his lips, his tongue, his fingers. By the time his hand trailed to her waist to unsnap her jeans, she thought she might explode.

He slid her jeans off, then peeled her panties down her legs. When lightning flashed, she could see his desire in his eyes, his need etched on his strained face. That she had this kind of effect on a man like Evan… She arched into him, watching every nuance on his face, exhilarated by her newfound power.

"Your body is so beautiful, Selena." She barely recognized his gravelly voice.

"It won't be in a few months," she said with a bold smile. "Enjoy it while you can."

"Oh, I am. But you'll be just as beautiful when that baby is out to here."

He held his hand in front of her now-flat belly and then slid it down between her legs, where her blood pulsed and her nerves screamed for contact. When he touched her intimately she nearly went through the ceiling.

"The curtains are wide open," she realized. The sofa faced the beach, front and center, and if anyone happened by, they'd get quite the eyeful.

"No one's out there. It's still pouring." He kissed his way up her jaw. "But if there was, they'd get the treat of a lifetime, let me tell you."

Selena turned to look behind her and Evan chuckled. "No one there, darlin'."

She raised her body enough to get at his pants and ripped the snap open. "Not fair for you to have so many clothes on," she said into his mouth. Instead of taking his shorts off all the way, she reached inside them and grasped him, closing her eyes as he pressed himself into her palm. "Do we need protection?" she asked, noticing her own voice sounded weird.

"Why? You can't get pregnant."

She laughed. "Ah. The upside of unplanned pregnancy, at last."

"I've been imagining for weeks how it'll feel to be inside you with nothing between us."

Selena held on to his length and directed it to her, taking him inside inch by inch.

"Yeah," he drawled. "That's exactly what I've been imagining. You feel so good."

She didn't know how he was talking and made it her goal to shatter his coherence. She took her time about it, though, teasing him, making him feel every single millimeter of movement, lifting her body almost completely off his, then slowly lowering herself to take him in completely. Over and over, until he finally grasped her hips and arched into her repeatedly.

"Wicked tease," he said as she lost the last bits of her control and their pace became mutually frantic.

Even as she climbed, aching for release, she never wanted to be without him, like this. Then she merely felt. And loved hearing her name on his lips as she bit his shoulder and plunged over the edge to total ecstasy.

They didn't move for several minutes afterward, just pressed light kisses to each other as their hearts pounded.

"Next time you don't get to wear your shorts," she finally said in a near whisper.

"Happy to oblige. How soon would you like the next time to be?"

She smiled into his lips. "Whenever you're up for it."

Evan stirred and stretched his sleep-deprived body, his eyes still shut. The light feminine scent was the first thing that jogged his memory and brought every amazing, earth-crashing moment of the night back to him. He reached for Selena's side of the bed but found only cool, empty sheets.

"Selena?" Maybe she was in the bathroom or making coffee. "Where are you, darlin'?"

He sat up, guessing by the complete silence she wasn't in the house. On the patio, maybe.

He surveyed the mess they'd made of the bed—sheets and blankets twisted and heaped mostly on the floor, pillows at odd angles. Even the fitted sheet had come loose from the mattress corner, making him smile.

He strolled into the bathroom, naked as the day he was born and already throbbing for Selena. He wasn't sure he'd ever get enough of that woman.

He splashed water on his face, then squeezed tooth-paste on his finger and ran it over his teeth.

His clothes were apparently still in the living room, although putting them back on was the last thing he wanted to do. Maybe she was up in her studio, taking advantage of the early light. He climbed the two flights of stairs, thinking the overstuffed chair in the studio would do just fine for what he had in mind.

There was no sign of her up there, though, either inside or out on the widow's walk. He stopped short of going outside to search up and down the beach, thinking the neighbors, whoever they were, might give Selena trouble if she had a naked man on her roof.

"Selena?" he called again, beginning to suspect maybe everything wasn't so happy for her. Their first morning after had been awkward, no doubt about it, but now they knew each other. There was nothing to be embarrassed about.

In the living room again, he pulled on his shorts, sans underwear, and, noticing the way the wind blew the sea grass, dragged his shirt over his head before going outside. The door was unlocked, so he was fairly sure he'd find her out here somewhere.

It didn't take long to spot her. She was a few hundred feet down the beach, about halfway between the house and the jetty at the south end of the island. Her hair blew freely behind her, and though he couldn't see her face, he'd recognize the sway of those hips from a mile away.

He caught up with her quickly, as she meandered along, seemingly lost in thought. That didn't bode well.

"What's a pretty girl like you doing all alone out here?" he asked when he was just a few feet behind her.

Her shoulders jerked, and she stopped and turned.

"I didn't mean to startle you."

"It's okay. I should be more aware of what's going on around me."

"You're lucky I have honorable intentions."

"Is that what you call it?" She tried to smile but it was a hollow attempt.

She'd pulled on a long, loose dress, gathered under her breasts, and thrown a denim jacket over it. Her hair was windblown, tangled, and she didn't wear any makeup. To him, she looked perfect.

"What's wrong, Selena?"

They started walking toward the south end of the island again, inches apart but not touching. The urge to take her hand was powerful, but she was emitting a serious don't-touch-me vibe.

"You regretting last night?" he prompted, needing to get the bad news out in the open so he could start convincing her everything would be okay.

"No."

He was surprised at her answer. "Good. To regret last night would be a crying shame."

She grinned shyly and he was yet again in awe of the two sides of Selena Jarboe.

"So are you going to tell me what's bugging you? Because after a night like that, I'm thinking it's not normal for a woman to run away."

"I didn't run away...." Her voice tapered off.

"That doesn't sound too convincing."

"Okay. I did, then."

They approached a wooden boardwalk perpendicular to the beach that led to the bay side of the island. It was only a couple hundred feet north of the jetty, bisecting the southern tip of the island. Selena stepped onto it and Evan followed her lead.

"Why did you run away?"

Their bare feet thudded on the wood that was still wet from the night's rain, with shallow puddles in some of the old, uneven slats. They were nearly halfway across the long walkway before she said a word.

"It's never going to work between us, Evan. Not for the long term. So while last night was incredible, I'm having a hard time. I guess I don't see what the point is. It's only going to make it worse later."

The relief he'd felt when she said she didn't regret last night took a nosedive. He frowned and shook his head.

"What makes you so sure that things can't work between us? In my book, they work pretty damn good."

"I'm not talking about sex now, Evan. That works. No question about it."

"Then what? What the hell are you talking about, Selena? Enlighten me, darlin', because I must be missing something."

CHAPTER SIXTEEN

SELENA FOCUSED on each wooden slat beneath her feet, a painful lump lodged in her throat and pressure building behind her eyes. This is where she wished with all her might that she was the kind of girl who could get involved with a man physically and keep her heart out of it. Men did it all the time—heck, she suspected *Evan* did it all the time. Women did, too, some of them. One of her friends from home was notorious for her parade of men, and Selena knew for a fact Jill had never had her heart broken. She just…wasn't the type. She would always be the breaker, not the breakee.

Selena had rarely been either, but she could see it from here—much more time with Evan and she would be devastated to lose him. Which was the whole point, wasn't it?

When they came to the end of the boardwalk, she trekked for the large boulders along the shore. A lone fisherman sat on one of the rocks farther down, but otherwise they had the area to themselves. Selena located a relatively smooth stone and carefully made her way toward it. Evan sat on an adjacent rock. The scowl on his face told her plenty about how well he was receiving what she was trying to say.

This was the hard part, the part she dreaded. She

wedged her elbows in her lap and leaned forward, staring at the water as it crashed against the boulders.

"My dad was FBI," she began, then took a fortifying breath. "When I was really young, all I knew was that my dad had an important job that required him to be gone a lot. I sensed the excitement of what he did, but it wasn't until I was in the first grade that I began to understand that every time he walked out that door, he could be risking his life. I remember so clearly how Brian Flanders skipped up to me on the playground one day and said, 'My daddy said it's lucky that your daddy hasn't got shot at his work.'"

She clenched her fists, still able to hear the singsong of his voice after all these years. "I was so mad at him, I yelled that he was stupid and he lied. The teacher heard me calling him stupid so I got in trouble. That night, I went home and asked my mom about it, because my dad was out of town, and she told me Dad had a very honorable job."

"Did she level with you then?"

"When I pestered her some more, she admitted his job could be dangerous. I don't think I was ever the same after that."

"That's rough. Seven years old?"

She nodded as tears flooded her eyes. "Every time he left for work, I'd hide in my mom's bed, scared to death I'd never see my dad again."

"What did your mom do?"

"She never said much. Just held me. Brushed my hair back. Mom things."

"You made her sound different the other day. Something about her screwing up."

"Back then it *was* different. *She* was different. Anyway, my point is that it was hell to live in that kind of fear, supportive family or not."

"Is your dad still an agent?"

Selena hesitated. "He died when I was twelve. On the job." She squeezed the words out before her throat swelled up, then choked on a sob.

Evan gently rubbed her leg. He didn't offer any token phrases of comfort, and Selena appreciated that. She wasn't looking for comfort—knew there was none. She was trying to make a point.

"I don't ever want my child to live like that, Evan. In constant fear. Daily stomachaches. I'll do everything I can to prevent him or her from losing a parent in an untimely death. A child should never be subjected to that kind of grief. And I know I couldn't take a loss like that again myself."

"You think something might happen to me," Evan said, his hand stilling on her thigh.

"It's hardly a far-fetched idea. You work in one of the most dangerous jobs out there."

"This isn't New York City, though. There's danger, but you have to understand it isn't what you see on TV."

"It doesn't matter. It only takes one bad day, one dangerous call."

"You have to look at the odds, Selena."

"Tell that to Frank Werschler's family." She'd lain awake several nights thinking about the man from the mural's wife and children, wondering what had become of them.

Evan stared out at a dolphin cruise boat in the distance for some time. Selena wished for the impossible—that he could somehow assure her he would always be safe. That he'd been thinking of getting out of the fire-fighting business and always wanted to be…a construction worker. Or about a thousand other jobs where he wouldn't lay his life on the line every day.

"It's a dangerous job sometimes. No way I can deny that. But we go through continuous training. We prepare for every possible type of situation we might run into. We do everything we can to stay safe."

"But firefighters still die."

"So do people who drive cars. Wall Street money guys. Farmers. People die, Selena, and it's always going to suck."

"Not good enough."

Evan turned his whole body to face her there on the rocks. He held both his hands up to hers and laced their fingers together. "There's never a guarantee, darlin'. Bad things happen."

"But I have to do everything I can to prevent my child and myself from experiencing those bad things."

"I'm going to be in this child's life. You can't prevent that, no matter how much it scares you."

"So you think it's okay to let the kid know you and love you when there's an above-average chance that you could die? Really?"

"I think growing up without a parent is as bad as losing one." He said it with such conviction that Selena narrowed her eyes, sensing there were things he hadn't told her.

His eyes didn't waver from hers.

"Yeah, I grew up without a father," he said, letting her hands go. "Since you've been so honest about your background, I'll tell you about mine."

"You don't have to, Evan," she said hesitantly. Nothing

he could say would change her mind, and though she did want to know more about him, what it came down to was that it wouldn't solve anything.

"I do." An edge of anger cut through his words. "You need to know where I'm coming from, because I'm not going to let this drop. I'm sorry as hell about your dad, and I understand why you don't want to worry about losing someone else you care about, assuming you would someday grow to care about me. No doubt your brother's accident tore you up even more."

Anguish jabbed at her with the raw memory of that phone call from one of the army officers. The excruciating hours they'd spent waiting to hear if Tom would pull through.

"I've never met my father." His voice broke on the last word and he was back to staring into the distance.

"He took off when my mom was pregnant with my sister and me. Didn't give half a damn about the two lives he helped create. Talking about him was never allowed. If you wanted to make my mom lose her cool, all you had to do was ask about him. She'd transform into a raging, angry woman."

"That had to be hard," Selena said quietly.

"It wasn't until I was about thirteen years old that I got the balls to ask her about him again."

"And? Did she tell you anything?"

Evan shook his head. "She explained, in no uncertain terms, that the man who had fathered us did not deserve to be thought of as our dad. To her, he was dead. She refused to give us his name or any other details. 'Just try to forget about him,' she'd tell us. 'He's not worth a second of your time.'"

Selena could see the sense in his mom's position. "She wanted to make it easier for you."

"There was nothing easy about growing up without a dad. I know she meant well, but kids are mean. The things they said to Mel and me…" He shook his head. "My mom never knew how bad it got."

"Lots of kids' parents are divorced," Selena said.

"And no one gave them any crap. It was that we didn't even know who our dad was. I had to sneak to look up the word *bastard* in the dictionary in my second-grade classroom because I somehow knew it would make my mother scream if I asked her."

"So you never found out who he was?"

"When I was old enough to figure out what to do, I got a copy of my birth certificate. She actually listed his name on it. It took me months but I eventually tracked him down."

"Did you meet him?"

"Never got the chance. He had a heart attack and died in prison."

"I'm sorry you never got to meet him."

"I'm not. Only reason I wanted to stand face-to-face with him was to unleash years of anger."

A large fishing boat passed relatively close to the shore and they watched it in silence. The captain waved and Evan nodded in response.

"I refuse to be anything like him, Selena," Evan said with quiet conviction. "My children will know who their father is and they'll know me, for better or worse."

Tears—of frustration, of hurt for a little boy named Evan, of feeling torn in half—blinded her. "I'm sorry. I can't take that risk."

"You can't just cut me out."

"If I think it's best for the baby, I can."

"I won't walk away, Selena."

"It's the only thing I can think of that might work."

"Work for who?" His voice climbed in volume. "You think you're the only one that matters?"

"No. We all matter, Evan," she growled, trying to keep her voice down. "But the baby has to come first."

She scrambled off the rocks, away from him, wishing she could scramble away from the entire dilemma, because she knew there was no perfect solution. As she hurried to the boardwalk, she wiped her eyes, trying to get rid of the tears that blurred her vision. She heard Evan behind her and sped up.

EVAN SAW the moment when Selena lost her footing. His heart stopped as she fell, and he saw the whole thing in slow motion. Even though he was only about twenty feet away when she went down, it seemed to take precious minutes to get to her.

Her head knocked against the railing and she landed on her tailbone with a thud. She lay there in silence, and awful thoughts tormented him in the two seconds it really took to reach her.

"Selena!" He knelt next to her and saw she was conscious.

Selena groaned and then rolled to her side away from him, curling into a fetal ball. Evan skittered around to the other side. She cried silently, her shoulders shaking.

"Selena, where does it hurt?"

She didn't answer right away.

He pulled out his cell phone and called for an ambulance. He thought he remembered that Scott and Luis were working today, though he'd be comfortable with any of the paramedics he knew.

"Head," she finally said. "Butt. Elbow."

He examined her arm and guessed her elbow had taken the brunt of the fall. "Do you think you're bleeding anywhere?" he asked.

She hesitated. Checked her hands and arms. Then shook her head. "I don't see any blood."

A siren wailed in the distance within a minute and a half. Selena opened her eyes and tried to sit up, but he gently held her down.

"You didn't have to call them. I'm fine."

"You hit your head and landed hard. You may feel fine, but we're going to be sure both you and the baby are okay."

"I fell on my butt. It hurts. That's all."

"I hope so. But you're not getting out of this."

The ambulance pulled up on the nearest road, which was a couple hundred yards away. Evan waved them down from his spot next to her at the end of the boardwalk.

Scott and Luis hurried toward them.

"These guys are the best, darlin'. Everything's okay."

"What the heck are you doing on this end, Drake?" Scott asked. "What's going on?"

Evan told them what had happened and what he'd already checked.

Scott asked her several questions and did a brief exam. When Evan mentioned her pregnancy, they decided to load her up and take her in, just to be safe.

"THE BABY LOOKS GOOD as far as I can tell right now," Dr. Martin said later, after they'd poked and prodded

Selena and run several different tests on both her and the fetus.

Evan had stayed by her side for every one of them, expecting her to order him out of the room. He wouldn't have gone, but she didn't ask. She seemed glad to have him there. He felt useless, which was frustrating as hell. All he could do was hold her hand.

"The bleeding concerns me a bit, but we'll watch it. It appears to have stopped for now and wasn't a large amount. The ultrasound doesn't show any hint of a rupture."

Selena closed her eyes in relief as Evan exhaled loudly.

"I want you to take it easy for the next three days. Bed rest."

Selena groaned.

"Lying down. No lifting, nothing strenuous, and that includes sexual activity." She looked at Evan pointedly and he shook his head.

"She'll do nothing, Doctor. I'll see to it."

"I have work to do," Selena said. "Deadlines."

"Not if you want to take care of this baby," the doctor said sternly. "I mean it, Selena. The deadlines will have to wait. I know it's hard to sit still but you can't push yourself. At all. Do you understand me?"

Selena's defensiveness relaxed and she nodded. "I understand."

Evan sat on the edge of her bed and caressed her arm. The only concrete damage they'd found was a mild concussion and the bleeding. But they'd checked the baby by ultrasound and the heart was still beating. He'd seen it with his own eyes.

It blew his mind to realize he'd be genuinely upset

if they lost the baby. That unborn tiny little fetus had turned both his and Selena's lives upside down, but he couldn't stomach the thought of losing it. How was that possible?

"Will you be taking her home?" Dr. Martin asked Evan.

"Yes, ma'am."

"Is there someone who can be with you continually for a couple of days, Selena? Just to make things easy on you, wait on you hand and foot?"

"I'll be okay," Selena said.

"I'll stay with her." He'd find someone to work his shift tomorrow. A couple of the guys owed him a favor.

The doctor watched Selena for a reaction. It took a few seconds, but Selena finally nodded.

"If there aren't any other options."

"I'm it, darlin'," he said, smiling.

Dr. Martin nodded and stood. "The nurse will be in with discharge directions in a few minutes. I want to see you in three days. Sooner, if you have any more bleeding or other problems." To Evan she added, "Take care of her."

"My pleasure," he responded. "Though probably not hers."

He hadn't forgotten where they'd left off before her fall, and he knew that with nothing but time on her hands, they'd be revisiting it before the three days were over.

CHAPTER SEVENTEEN

SELENA LAY ON her couch, knowing she was being a complete and utter pain in the ass. Okay, and maybe she was doing it on purpose. At least a little.

Her head throbbed with every beat of her heart and she refused to take any pain meds for it. The doctor had assured her it wouldn't hurt the baby but Selena wasn't taking any chances. She'd heard Dr. Martin's mention of the possibility of the placenta ripping away from the uterine wall. She'd do anything to improve the baby's odds.

The front door opened and Evan strode into the living room of the beach house.

"Everything okay?" he asked.

"Nothing's changed."

He was being a rock star, verging on sainthood. Fetching whatever she asked for, dealing with her extreme grumpiness.

"Dinner is served," he said, setting a large paper bag on the end table. "Spicy lasagna, bread sticks and salad. Double serving of Italian dressing on the side." He held up a smaller plastic bag from the grocery store. "Half gallon of butter pecan ice cream, going to the freezer now."

"Thank you," she said. She annoyed even herself with her mood swings, but dammit, she was ticked off. She really did have work that needed to be done—like, yesterday. That she could even think about work after her fall... It had occurred to her that several of her problems would be solved if she were to lose this baby.

As soon as the thought had crossed her mind, the guilt had nearly suffocated her. What kind of a mother was she going to be? Was she going to be as bad as her own mom?

Unfortunately for Evan, he'd been the one to receive the brunt of her anger, guilt, worry, and the other two hundred emotions that'd stormed through her over the course of the day.

She slowly sat up and propped an extra cushion behind her back, then reached behind her head to grab the bag of food.

"Stop. I've got it," Evan said as he came back into the room.

"You're going to stop me from lifting a measly bag of food?"

"No. I'm going to stop you from dumping my dinner all over the floor. I've been breathing it in for the past twenty minutes and I plan to enjoy every last bite."

As he spoke, he set the take-out containers on the floor next to him, unwrapped the plastic fork for her and scooped the lasagna onto two plates. He handed one to her.

"Thank you, Evan."

"No worries. I'm starving, too."

"I mean for everything. I've been unbearable today and yet here you are, still taking care of me."

"Like I said, I'm just hungry." He grinned and sat on the floor, his back against the couch.

"Yeah. And I'm a good candidate for motherhood."

He'd just shoved a bite into his mouth and turned to study her, saying around the food, "Where the hell did that come from?"

"The heart." She took her first bite of pasta and tried to ignore him.

"We talked about that, Selena. If you want to be a good mom, you will be."

She took her time chewing, then reached for the glass of water he'd gotten for her earlier. "You think my mom just stopped wanting to be good?"

"What happened with her, Selena? What went wrong between you two?"

Selena closed her eyes and shook her head. "I wish I knew," she said softly. "After my dad was shot, she was never the same. It's like she went cold."

"You could never be cold."

"I used to think that about her."

He watched her for several seconds. "Have you ever talked to her about it?"

"We don't have much of a talking-about-things relationship."

"Maybe you should try. For your own peace of mind."

Selena hated every bit of this conversation so she didn't respond.

"I don't want you to stay here tomorrow," she said after several minutes of silence. "You need to work."

"Too late. I got Rafe to take my shift."

"I'll be fine by myself. Really."

"Then I'll stay out of the room so you won't know I'm here."

"Evan, I mean it. I don't want to owe you any more than I already do...."

"Owe me? Seriously? Tell me you didn't really mean to say that."

"I meant it."

"How many times do I have to tell you...you don't owe me. For anything. You have to carry the kid. The least I can do is get you dinner or keep you company when you can't move."

Selena was about to disagree when someone knocked on the door.

Evan set his food on the floor and got up to answer it. "Expecting anyone?"

She shook her head. "Maybe it's Macey."

"She has to close the bar tonight."

Selena shrugged. She didn't really care who it was, as long as Evan made the intruder go away. Fatigue was setting in and she wasn't sure she could even finish her meal.

"Can I help you?" she heard Evan ask.

"I'm looking for my daughter. Is Selena here?"

No. *No way.* Her mother was *not* really here.

"You're Selena's mother?" There was surprise in his voice and she knew it was because her mom looked young enough to be her sister, thanks to plastic surgery.

"Where is my daughter?"

Nice manners, Mom.

"I'm in here! Evan, go ahead and let her in."

Her mom barreled down the hallway, heels clicking on the tile floor.

"Thank you, God." Clara Cambridge-Jarboe was dressed in black slacks and a burgundy cashmere sweater. In full makeup and three-inch heels, she toted a Prada purse big enough to stow a small child. The only telltale sign that she'd just traveled across the country was that her hair was less than perfect, with a couple of auburn strands out of place. "Now that I've laid eyes on you, I'll return in a moment."

Before Selena could say a word, her mother had clicked back down the hall out of sight. Evan appeared at the entrance to the living room, his eyes narrowed.

"That's your mother."

It wasn't really phrased as a question but Selena nodded anyway.

"She arrived in a stretch limo. Won't even fit in the driveway."

Selena rolled her eyes but wasn't surprised. Her mother would sooner fly directly back home than be caught in a regular taxi.

EVAN STARED at Selena but she didn't say a word. He went back to the door, completely baffled by the woman who'd just shown up. She was making her way toward the house again, climbing the single flight of stairs from the driveway, as out of place here on San Amaro Island as a black stallion among dairy cows. She was dressed to the hilt and though Evan didn't know the first thing about ladies' handbags, the one she carried looked like it cost more than his truck.

Then the limo driver appeared, loaded down with three enormous bags. He was following her to the house, Evan realized. And the woman didn't appear the least bit bothered that she was only carrying her purse while the driver could barely walk.

It struck him that the pregnant woman on the couch was more of a stranger to him than he'd ever guessed.

Selena's mother waltzed through the door and down

the hallway to her daughter, barely acknowledging Evan. He went out to help the driver with his load. He took the biggest suitcase from him and groaned as he lifted it. That thing had to weigh close to seventy-five pounds. What the hell did the woman have in there? And how long did she intend to stay?

"You may set my bags by the stairs, please."

Evan refused to let his jaw drop, though it took serious effort. He glanced over at Selena, but she didn't appear to have noticed anything out of the ordinary.

Didn't that just speak volumes.

Who was this woman he'd thought he was getting to know for the past few weeks? Who was her mother? And maybe more to the point, who did she *think* she was?

The woman handed the limo driver a bill—a large bill—and the guy left.

"What are you doing here, Mom?" Selena said tiredly.

"I could ask you the same." Her mother sat pristinely on the old armchair closest to the couch. "It's been almost two months, Selena. Do you know how sick with worry I've been?"

Evan still stood near the stairway, trying to absorb this new facet of the woman he was trying to marry.

"Evan, this is my mother, Clara Cambridge-Jarboe. Mom, Evan Drake."

Mrs. Cambridge-Jarboe turned and offered a hand to him. "It's a pleasure to meet you."

"Likewise, ma'am." He shook her hand, then moved both lasagna plates to the end table. He sat on the edge of the couch, by Selena's knees, not really sure how he fit in.

"Who told you where to find me?" Selena asked her mom, clearly upset.

"No one. At first I assumed you were traveling but after so long, I figured the only place you could be was the beach house your dad left you. I came as soon as I found replacements for my social commitments."

Now Evan's mouth did gape open. Selena owned this house? Its value had more zeroes than he'd ever see in his lifetime. What a fool he'd been, trying to help her with a three-hundred-dollar doctor's bill.

"So you found me. What do you want?" Selena asked.

"I want you to come home."

He felt Selena's body tense behind him. He whispered to her to relax. Getting upset wouldn't help anyone. Least of all the baby.

"Are you kidding? I can't relax," she said aloud. "I'm not going back to Boston, Mom."

"It's your home, Selena. You belong there."

"This is my home now."

"Your brother asks about you every time he calls."

Low blow, Evan thought.

"All he has to do to talk to me is come home. Permanently."

"I don't want to argue about this again. That's not what I'm here for."

"Right. You already said what you're here for and I'm not coming home. So you can leave now. You've done your matronly duty."

Hurt flickered over Mrs. Cambridge-Jarboe's face.

"I just flew across the country. I plan to stay here a few days."

"You cut me off from our money and then expect me to put you up here?"

"I was just trying to get you to come home, honey. The house is awfully quiet."

"An iPod is cheaper than a plane ticket to Texas."

"That's not fair, Selena."

Selena pulled out the extra cushion from behind her back and reclined on the sofa. Her lips moved slightly and it took several seconds for Evan to realize she was counting to herself.

"I'm sorry, Mom. It's not a good time for me. I really need to rest."

"You look pale. Is everything okay?"

"Depends on how you define *okay*," Selena muttered.

Evan took Selena's hand, her very apparent fatigue worrying him. "Does she know anything that's happened?" he asked her quietly.

"I do not," her mom said. "Yet."

"You need to tell your mom what's going on," Evan said. "I can leave the room or I can stay. But you have to tell her."

"Selena, *what* is this man talking about?"

Selena closed her eyes, frowning. As she inhaled, he could see her chest rise slowly. He gave her hand a gentle squeeze.

"Where to start?" Selena said flippantly, opening her eyes.

"You decide," he replied, planning to stay with her unless she asked for privacy.

"I don't understand what's happening," her mom said. "Are you involved with my daughter?"

Involved was one word for it.

"Do we have to do this right now? For real?" Selena asked Evan.

"Get it over with. Then sleep."

Selena stared at the ceiling. "Well, Mom…I'm pregnant."

Her mother gasped. Loudly. "Selena?"

"Knocked up. Your grandbaby is due June twenty-eighth. If it makes it through the week."

Silence fell over the room for several seconds. "What do you mean, if it makes it through the week?"

Selena explained about her fall and related the doctor's prognosis.

"Oh, honey…you've been handling this all by yourself?"

"Do I look like I'm alone?"

Clara turned her attention to Evan, studied him. "Thank you, Evan," she said finally. "Are you the baby's father?"

"Yes, ma'am. I've been trying to convince Selena to marry me."

"I see," was all she said, and her tone was indifferent.

"Stop planning the engagement party, Mom. We're not getting married."

"I wasn't planning. I was trying to process everything you've just told me. How could you not call me? I would've sent you money for the doctor if I'd known."

"Oh, no. Evan?" Selena said, paling. "I didn't think about that.… How big a check did you have to write at the hospital this morning?"

"I didn't pay for any of it. They'll bill you. I don't know how much."

"I'll leave you money for it," her mom said, and she started digging through her handbag.

"I'll figure out how to handle it, Mom. I've got an income now."

"You...what?"

"I have a job. Two jobs, really."

"My God, Selena. What has happened to you?" She said it as if Selena had announced she was joining the circus.

"What did you expect me to do when I couldn't withdraw money to buy food?"

"I already told you. I expected you to come home."

Selena looked as if she was about to snap a reply but she stopped herself.

"I think it would be best if Selena got some sleep now. Stress is the last thing she needs," Evan said, taken aback by the whole exchange. Hell, by the whole visit and everything it had revealed so far.

Selena looked at him in gratitude.

"I'm sorry," her mother said. "You're right, Evan. What can I do to help, honey?"

"Nothing right now," Selena said. "Actually..."

"Just say it. Whatever you need."

What had happened to the woman who was horrified her daughter had taken a job?

"Since you're in town, could you stay here tomorrow so Evan can go to work?"

"Of course."

"I've already made arrangements, Selena," Evan told her. "I said I would stay with you and I meant it." He had lots to process about the things he'd learned tonight, but he was a man of his word.

"I'll be here already," Mrs. Cambridge-Jarboe said.

"Nothing to worry about. You can visit if it makes you feel better but I can handle the job."

"Or you two could both get lost and give me some peace." Selena pressed her fingers to her temples.

"What fun would that be?" Evan asked.

"I can become better acquainted with Evan," her mom said.

"Maybe I can join you," Selena said drily.

"I'll pretend I didn't hear that," her mom said, standing. "Which room may I sleep in?"

"Take your pick. I don't know what condition they're in."

"Don't worry, honey. I'll take care of it."

"The bed might need to be changed, Mom. It might still smell like smoke."

Her mom's eyes widened. "What else have I missed, Selena?"

She told her mom about the fire, downplaying it.

"I'll check the sheets," Evan said as he stood. "Please. Relax."

"You don't have to change my mother's bed."

"Shh. Rest. Where are the extras?"

"In the hall closet on the second floor. This is ridiculous." Selena started to get up.

"Down," Evan said with a gentle but firm hand to her shoulder. "I've got it."

Mrs. Cambridge-Jarboe was halfway up the stairs. Her luggage still sat on the entry floor, waiting for someone to carry it upstairs. He picked up the largest bag and took it with him. He found her in the second room on the left, which overlooked the beach. She'd already pulled back the covers and was running her hand over the sheet. She bent down to smell it, then nodded.

"Bad?" he asked.

"Needs to be changed. But I'll do it."

Hallelujah.

"I'll say good-night, then. I'm going to help Selena to her bed before I leave."

"Good night."

There was no need to help Selena do anything, Evan realized when he came downstairs to an empty couch. Her bedroom door was ajar and he tapped on it. When she didn't answer, he pushed the door open a little more and looked in. The lights were out and he could barely see her. She didn't stir. He could've walked out and she wouldn't have known the difference, but he was compelled to go into the room.

He stared at her face as she slept, wondering what other major parts of her life she'd neglected to mention. Was he making the mistake of his life in trying to get her to marry him?

CHAPTER EIGHTEEN

AFTER THREE DAYS of bed rest, Selena was climbing the walls. She'd been horizontal for so long that she could no longer sleep, even though it was just after seven in the morning.

Her appointment with Dr. Martin was in less than two hours so she might as well shower.

She'd had minor spotting the day after the fall and had worried herself into a fit, but it had stopped soon after, just as her mother had somehow managed to calm her down. Other than that, the only problem was achiness from the fall itself, and she'd been assured that was normal. She had high hopes for a good report on the baby and really hoped she could get back to a normal life now. Or what had become her new normal.

She was almost done with the firefighter mural and had been working on the design for the next one, at the nature reserve. If she didn't get back to it soon, she'd fall way behind.

After a long shower, she slowly got dressed in real clothes for the first time since her wipeout. She sat on her bed to dry her hair, worn-out from these small efforts.

By the time she had eaten a bagel with peanut butter, it was eighty-thirty. Her mother hadn't come downstairs yet, was most likely still asleep. The appointment wasn't until nine. Macey was supposed to pick her up in fifteen minutes, so Selena decided to wait outside.

Stepping out the front door, she stopped short. Evan sat in his truck, engine off. His head was reclined and his eyes were closed.

She walked around to his side and tapped on the window. He jolted awake.

"Hey," he said as he opened the door.

"What are you doing here?" she asked.

"Your appointment's at nine, right?"

"Yes. But Macey's taking me."

"Selena, I want to be there. This is important."

"I figured you were at work."

"I got off at seven. You know that."

"You look tired." A close look at his face revealed shadows under his eyes.

"Long night."

She pressed her hand over her racing heart. "Bad call?"

"Just lots of little ones. I think we had four after midnight. We'd get ten or fifteen minutes' sleep and then another alarm would go off."

"But you're safe."

"Of course I'm safe. And flattered you care."

"You should go home and go to bed."

"No. Whether the news is good or bad today, it's big. I'm going with you."

"What should I do about Macey?"

"Call her and tell her I've got it covered, or she can go with us."

Selena took her phone out of her purse, knowing it was pointless to argue. "I'll see if I can catch her."

DR. MARTIN WAS running behind and it was all Evan could do to stay awake in the waiting room.

"Go ahead and sleep," Selena said, touching his thigh and having more of an effect on him than she could probably ever guess. Maybe lust could wake him up.

The nurse finally called Selena's name and they both stood and followed her to the same ultrasound room they'd been in at the first appointment.

The nurse hurried through several questions and said the doctor would be in right away. Her brisk manner unnerved Evan, as if she expected bad news and didn't want to be cheerful.

"Turn around," Selena said to him, holding the sheet in front of her.

He stared at her for a moment. Was she kidding?

"Evan."

"I've seen all that before, darlin'."

"Not here. Please?"

Slowly, he bent over and put his hands over his eyes.

"Thank you."

She undressed in record time and secured the sheet around her waist. Evan might've teased her if he hadn't been so tense and ready to get this over with.

It seemed as if they sat there, in silence, for an hour, but in reality only about eight minutes had passed. Dr. Martin knocked softly on the door and got straight to business, which Evan appreciated. There was a time for chitchat, and waiting to find out if your baby was still alive was definitely not it.

"I'm going to see if we can find the heartbeat with the Doppler first," the doctor said. "It's less invasive. But keep in mind it may be a little early in the pregnancy to hear it. So if we can't, no panicking."

She lifted Selena's shirt a few inches and lowered the sheet to reveal her lower abdomen. After rubbing gel over the area, she held an instrument on Selena's skin and moved it around. It sounded like the sea in a seashell through a microphone, but Evan didn't hear anything resembling a heartbeat.

The doctor probed for a couple minutes and frowned. "Okay. We'll do another vaginal ultrasound."

She was all business as she rolled the equipment closer and put gloves on.

Evan leaned his head close to Selena and kissed her cheek. "Doing okay?" he asked.

She nodded, looking slightly green. "You?"

"Not in the least."

"Almost ready," Dr. Martin said. She turned the lights out and started the procedure.

Once again, Evan couldn't make heads or tails or heartbeats out of anything on the screen. Seconds ticked by as the doctor searched and Selena cringed. He closed his eyes, trying to prepare himself for bad news.

"There it is," the doctor said, her relief evident. "That little heart is still beating away."

"Yes!" Evan said. He brought Selena's hand to his mouth and kissed it.

"Everything's okay?" Selena asked in a small voice.

"That heartbeat is exactly what we wanted to see, sweetie. I'm going to glance around a little more but your baby looks good."

Selena finally exhaled and smiled up at Evan. He kissed her again and thought how bizarre it was that they were so relieved. If someone had told him three months ago he would be here praying for a heartbeat, he would've said they were out of their mind.

"The placenta appears to be in good shape," Dr. Martin said. "That was our main concern. Baby's growth is perfect." She wrote something on Selena's chart. "Due date is still right on target."

After a few more minutes of viewing the blob parts on the screen, the doctor finished up and turned it off.

"Everything's okay, but I want you to take it easy for another day or two. No long walks or vigorous activity. Understand?"

Selena nodded. "I don't have to stay in bed, right?"

"Right. But naps are your friend." The doctor fixed Evan with a stare. "You going to see to it she lies low?"

"Yes, ma'am."

"If you have any more spotting, I want you back in here or the E.R. right away. Same with abdominal cramping or pain. Got it?"

"Got it," Selena said. "Thank you, Doctor."

"Okay. No more romantic walks on a wet boardwalk, you two."

Selena met Evan's eyes as they both recalled how unromantic that walk had been.

"Anything else?" Evan asked.

"I'll see you at your regular appointment. Take care."

"So," SELENA SAID when they were back in the truck. "Sounds like we're going to have a baby after all."

"Sounds like it. You still okay with that?"

"Strangely...yes. I think I'd be at least a little upset

if something bad happened. How's that for sick and twisted?"

"Pretty darn twisted." He leaned his head back and drummed the steering wheel with his index fingers. "Me, too."

Selena looked at him sharply. Studied his profile and felt the punch to her gut yet again at how good-looking he was. What surprised her even more was his heart. His looks and charm had suckered her in that first night they'd met, and she'd never suspected he would turn out to be such a decent man deep down. She wished like crazy he wasn't so good, didn't thrive on helping people day in and day out. Maybe if he wasn't, she could handle loving him.

Not that she did. Love him. She couldn't. *Would not.*

"I know you're practically sleepwalking, but would you mind if we made one stop on the way home?"

"The good news woke me up. I'm fine. Just tell me where."

Selena directed him to one of the many strip malls on the island's main street. He pulled up in front of Abuela's Consignments and stopped the engine. He looked at her suspiciously.

"Not a shopper?" she said, trying to stifle a grin.

"You're supposed to be taking it easy."

"This will take ten minutes at the most."

He checked his watch. "You've got ten. Let's go."

Selena didn't waste any time. They walked inside and she looked around for the section she needed.

"Hola," an elderly woman said from a few feet away. "Can I help you?"

Selena saw what she wanted, smiled and said, "Not yet."

She took Evan's hand and dragged him to the back of the store, where there were several racks and shelves of baby clothes.

"Selena," he said when he realized her intention. "Are you sure about this?"

"I'm not sure about anything, but this is the first time I've been in the least bit excited. I think we should celebrate by buying the baby's first outfit."

Evan gradually smiled as he stared at her, then nodded.

Selena browsed through the rack closest, which happened to be full of pink and lavender, ruffles, dresses, bows, kitties and bunnies.

"He'll be scarred for life," Evan said.

"He?"

"You think it's a girl?"

"No idea. I haven't thought that far." She moved on to the next rack, which had sleepers in all colors. She pulled one of the minihangers off the rack and held up a tiny long-sleeved, footed pajama in light green.

Evan tilted his head. "Too hot for June?"

"Maybe," Selena said. "It's so little." She checked for a size. "Three to six months. They start smaller than this?"

"And grow big fast. At least Henry has."

"That was big?" She stuck the green sleeper back on the rack. "I don't know about this. Maybe it's a bad idea."

Evan wandered to the next rack and Selena searched for a lighter sleeper, trying to ignore her fear.

"Three minutes left," Evan said, but she noticed he was still searching through baby clothes.

"I've got it." Selena pulled out a fuzzy yellow sleeper with an all-over panda-bear print.

"Got mine," Evan said.

Intrigued, and touched that he was picking something out, too, she took her choice to the rack where he stood.

"You're kidding, right?"

"What? No way! This is it. Works for either gender."

Selena eyed the onesie, shaking her head. It was pure white with a fire truck embroidered across the chest. Around the graphic, it said, "My daddy's truck is bigger than your daddy's truck."

"It's perfect. Let's go." Evan led her by the hand and to the checkout counter near the door before she could voice her misgivings.

"What did you select?" the shopkeeper asked as they laid their choices on the counter. "Ooh, so cute." She moved them toward the cash register to ring them up. "Cash or credit?"

"Plastic," Evan said.

"Cash," Selena said at the same time.

"I've got it." Evan took his wallet out of his back pocket.

"This was my idea. I'll get them."

"Oh," Evan said, suddenly looking annoyed. "How could I forget? You're rich enough to buy the entire strip mall."

"They're five dollars apiece, Evan. Don't be like that."

"Like what?" He took a card out of his wallet.

"We'll pay for them separately," he told the woman, who watched them with undisguised interest.

They purchased each outfit—separately—in silence and returned to the truck.

"Clearly, we have something we need to discuss," Selena said after they were in.

Evan leaned his elbow on his door. "Were you ever planning to tell me you're a high-society princess? What do they call them? Debutantes?"

"Why are you so angry? You never asked about my family's finances."

"It didn't cross my mind that you might be richer than God."

"I, personally, have been flat broke."

"So you said."

"You heard my mom. She cut me off to get me back to Boston. I left home with two thousand dollars cash, never dreaming I wouldn't be able to get more."

"Are you listening to yourself? Two grand? In cash?"

Selena narrowed her eyes. "What's this about, Evan? Get to the point."

"The point is that I've been concerned about taking care of this child financially. I gave up plans to buy the boat of my dreams because I was worried about paying for a crib and a rocking chair and the million other expenses a child brings."

"This is about a boat?"

"No, it's not about a goddamn boat, Selena. It's about me not knowing a thing about you."

"Well, there you go. Best reason yet to stop trying to get me to marry you. Go buy your boat."

Evan started the truck and drove to the beach house without another word.

"Coming in to say hello to the high-society queen?" Selena asked when he stopped in her driveway.

"I don't think so."

Selena stared at him, her head spinning from the crazy roller coaster of a morning. "See you." She climbed out and went into the house. It took more than a little effort for her to avoid looking back at him.

CHAPTER NINETEEN

EVAN HAD BLOWN IT the other day at the consignment store and he knew it. What he didn't know was how to fix it.

"What's up?" Derek said as Evan entered the Shell Shack just after it opened.

"Hey, Gus." Evan sat on a stool at the counter next to Derek's uncle.

"Howdy, boy." Gus gave him a wrinkly grin.

"Where's Macey today?" Evan asked Derek.

"Tied up with meetings for her foundation. I'm holding the fort here."

"He's fixin' to try, anyway," Gus muttered good-naturedly.

"Might be a busy one," Evan said. "Haven't had weather this good for a couple weeks."

"Bring it on," Derek said. "Nearly eighty degrees in November. We could use it." He helped himself to a Coke from the fountain. "What can I get you?"

"Usual. Burger, loaded. Fries with cheese. Bottle of Bud."

Derek got the beer and set it in front of Evan then went to the back to start the food. Several other people sauntered in and a couple of them came to the counter to place an order.

"They're doing okay with this place, aren't they?"

Gus said with a hint of pride. "'Course, Macey can take most of the credit."

Evan chuckled, looking around them. "Only a few empty seats in the slow season. I'd say that's awfully good. They kind of act as a team, don't they?"

Gus nodded. "She's just what he needed. And the bar."

Derek handled it well as they sat there watching, Evan distracted the whole time by thoughts of Selena.

After orders had been taken and Evan's food was ready, Derek leaned on the counter and stole a fry. "What's happening today?"

Evan took a long drink. "Damage control."

"Uh-oh," Gus said.

"What'd you do? Piss off Selena?"

"Spoken like a man of experience," Evan said.

"Hell, yeah. Been there. Will be there again. So what happened?"

"Join the brotherhood, boys," Gus said.

Evan chewed his burger. "Found out Selena is stinking rich."

"Hallelujah." Gus reached over the bar for a toothpick.

"How stinking rich?" Derek asked.

"She *owns* the beach house she's staying in. Not her family. Her."

"How does she own *that?*"

"Her dad left it to her."

"You just found all this out?"

"Didn't have any idea. A couple weeks ago she'd been planning to go to the free health clinic because she was broke, supposedly. She drives a Saturn, man. Hell, she's been working two jobs."

Gus picked at his teeth and shook his head, amused.

Derek crossed his arms. "Now that you say it, though, I can see it. She's got a manner about her that tells you she doesn't eat beans and weenies for dinner."

"She's got...class, I guess you'd call it. But she's down-to-earth," Evan admitted. "Compared to her mother."

"Is mom a snob?"

Evan told them about the limo, the driver, the luggage. "Who wears pearls for a cross-country flight to the beach?"

Derek chuckled. "Your future mother-in-law, if you get your way."

"You got your hands full, son," Gus said.

"What the hell am I getting into? What happened to my life?"

"Sometimes I shake my head when I realize in a few months I'll be a married man," Derek commiserated. "I imagine Macey will want babies soon after. Downright crazy, man."

"You don't seem too worried about it," Evan said, grinning.

"Do him some good." Gus nodded and crossed his arms, chewing on the end of the toothpick.

"Wouldn't change a thing," Derek said. "So what'd you do to tick off your rich girl?"

"Acted like a son of a bitch when she wanted to pay for a five-dollar baby outfit."

Derek nodded sympathetically. "How you going to fix it?"

"Wish I knew. I need to make it up to Selena. Scoring some points with her mom wouldn't be a bad plan, either. Selena won't listen to her opinion, but I'd like to get along with the ice queen if we're going to be family."

"You're still thinking marriage, then?"

"Nothing's changed there."

"Hoo, dog," Gus howled.

Derek studied Evan. "You care more than you're letting on. It's not just about the kid anymore, is it?"

Evan stared into his half-full bottle. "It's not just the kid. But I don't know what the hell it is."

A customer came up to the counter to order drinks and Derek served her and collected her money. He returned to Evan, wiping his hands on the towel over his shoulder.

"So. Selena and her mom," Derek said. "You play things their way. Take them out for a fancy dinner or something. Wine and dine both of them. Throw in some groveling in private."

"That's what I'm thinkin'," Gus agreed.

Evan nodded. He just needed to figure out the wine-and-dine thing. He was a burger and beer man. Selena's mom was more caviar and champagne. There had to be a way to bring their worlds together without acting like something he wasn't.

SELENA COULDN'T help but wonder what Evan was up to.

Still angry, she hadn't been thrilled to hear from him, but for once he'd called her in advance and asked if he could take her out. Her and her mom. She was just curious enough to acquiesce, surprised her mother had agreed to go, as well. Clara had never been the type of mom who liked to spend time with Selena and her friends. Not in the past decade and a half.

Evan had given Selena very little information about where they were going or what they were doing, saying only to wear layers and bring a jacket. They'd likely be gone for a few hours.

Clara was fluttering importantly around the house, trying on the resort wear she'd bought for her trip to San Amaro, even though it was completely inappropriate. As if this was a cruise ship or something. Selena just hoped she would behave herself around Evan.

Selena wore jeans, a fitted button-down blouse that was only a little snug in the lower abdomen and a casual patchwork sweater. She carried a loose-knit sweater-jacket. She doubted she'd need the jacket—her body temperature had seemed to go up about ten degrees in the past month or so. Her hair was pulled back at her nape in a low ponytail. She rushed to throw on some makeup before he arrived.

A few minutes later, Evan knocked on the door and Selena let her mother answer it. She refused to be excited to see him, not after the way they'd left things the other day. He obviously had some deep issues about her family's bank account—even though she'd been cut off from it.

"Selena, are you ready?" her mother called.

She gathered her purse and jacket and steeled herself against any reaction to him.

Didn't work.

When she went out to the living room, she caught her breath as she laid eyes on him. He was dressed in dark, worn jeans that molded to his thighs and butt as if they'd been stitched around him and a navy blue T-shirt that stretched across his wide, muscled chest. He leaned against the wall in the hallway, his cornflower-blue eyes glued to her, only a sexy hint of a smile on his face.

"Hi," she said, doing her best to pretend she wasn't affected by him in the least.

"Hi. Glad y'all are able to go out with such short notice."

"Are you going to tell us where we're going now?"

"That'd ruin the surprise, wouldn't it?"

"I'm okay with that."

"Selena, when did you forget how to have fun?" her mother asked as she pulled on a caramel suede jacket.

"A few weeks ago, when I found out I was pregnant."

"You might enjoy this if you let yourself," Evan said. His hand on the small of her back, he guided her toward the door behind her mother.

They were hit by blinding sunlight when they stepped outside.

"I forgot my sunglasses," Clara said. "I'll just be a moment." She went back inside while Selena took her own sunglasses out of her bag and put them on.

"I hope you know what you're doing," she said as they neared her truck. "If she isn't happy, no one will be happy."

"Don't worry so much," Evan said. "I'll win her over."

"Is that what this is about? Because if so…"

She was about to say there was no point because he wasn't going to win her mother over. Selena had been trying for years. Her mom hurried out the door, though, and Selena kept the comment to herself.

"Just want to get to know your family," Evan said,

close to her ear. "Hope you don't mind riding in the backseat. It's small but we're only going a few miles."

"It's fine," Selena said, following him to the passenger door, where he slid the seat forward and helped her in. Her belly had seemingly swollen overnight and for the first time, she could feel it as she bent forward. Just barely, but it was there, bigger than usual. She put her hand on her abdomen as she sat back on the narrow seat, trying to imagine what it would be like in several weeks to feel the baby actually move. Too weird.

Evan helped her mom up to the front seat, then went around to the driver's side and got in. An uneasy silence settled over them as Evan backed out, and Selena thought how none of them had a single thing in common. This outing, whatever it was, could—and likely would—turn out to be a nightmare.

Evan surprised her, though. He asked her mom questions about places she'd traveled. Told her about the island's history and explained some of the sites as they drove by. Her mom loved talking about travel and seemed interested in everything he said. The five-minute ride went much better than Selena had expected. That was a start.

Evan turned into a mostly deserted parking lot on the bay side of the island. The shore was across a narrow street and was lined with small businesses, most of them bars and restaurants capitalizing on the waterside location.

"You're taking us to a bar," Selena guessed, hoping to God she was wrong.

"I'm taking you to the San Amaro Marina."

They walked three abreast on the wide sidewalk that wound behind the businesses and led to the docks.

Selena's fingers itched as she took in the rows of boats, most of them gargantuan, some sailboats and lots of yachts. She'd have to paint this colorful scene soon.

The air buzzed with activity as people prepared to take their vessels out or brought them back in. Sunbathers stretched out on decks in the afternoon sun; sport fishermen fiddled with their equipment, a couple of kids spit over the railing of one boat into the bay. Everyone seemed in a celebratory mood because of the perfect unseasonable weather.

"I never knew there was so much money lurking about on San Amaro," Selena said as they trekked out onto one of the main heavy-duty docks. "I don't remember any of this from when I was a kid."

"It's fantastic," her mom said, and Selena wished she meant the setting and the boats, not the money.

"What are we doing?" Selena asked.

"You'll see." Evan walked ahead, leading them onto dock number two.

"Beautiful," Selena's mom said as they wandered past yachts that could probably sleep a small army and sailboats with towering masts.

Evan turned onto one of the narrow perpendicular docks, his attention riveted on the boat to his right. It was one of the smaller ones in the marina yet still big enough for a large group. The name painted on the side was *Hot Water*.

"It's ours for the afternoon if you ladies are game."

Clara eyed the boat critically and Selena held her breath, waiting for her to pass judgment.

"Are we trespassing?" Selena asked, only half joking.

Evan climbed onto the boat and turned to help

them. "Belongs to the fire chief," he explained when Selena didn't move. "He gave me permission, Miss Worrywort."

Her mother took Evan's hand and climbed aboard. She made herself at home, exploring the deck and the view from every side without hesitation.

"Do you know how to drive it?" Selena asked, still on the dock.

The look he gave her said the question was insulting. Finally she gave in and joined them.

Evan showed them around. The interior was even bigger than Selena would've guessed, with three bedrooms, or staterooms as Evan informed her they were called, a galley, dining area and living room with a big flat-screen TV and comfortable-looking furniture. After seeing this thing, Selena couldn't imagine the insides of the larger vessels out there.

"What do you think?" Evan asked them.

Selena waited. Her mom would no doubt say exactly what she thought, good or bad.

"I've always wanted a boat." Clara sat down on the overstuffed sofa in the living room. "I'd probably prefer a sailboat—there's something so romantic about riding the wind."

"Why haven't you just bought a sailboat, then?" Selena asked. Money couldn't be what held her back, and usually when her mom wanted something, she bought it.

"It's a large commitment. There's just always been other things to consider. Trips. The house here. Nantucket. Cars."

"I've been sailing a couple of times," Evan said. "Could definitely see the allure."

"This isn't bad," Selena's mom said. "It should do just fine for an afternoon on the water."

Selena restrained herself from rolling her eyes. Now that they had the queen's blessing…

"Is the boat you wanted to buy like this one?" Selena asked, belatedly recalling what he'd said during their argument.

"Older and smaller. Just one stateroom and one head. Only thirty-five feet. But the same type. It's called a trawler yacht. Patterned after a fishing trawler but made into a luxury boat."

"Used for fishing?" Selena asked.

"You could fish off it but it's best for cruising. A lot of people live on them as they go from one port to another. Kind of the RV of the ocean."

Selena nodded, trying to imagine that kind of life-style. "Where are you taking us today?"

"Thought we'd go out on the Gulf and have a picnic. I stocked the fridge and the bar. I'll have you home by early evening."

"Will you make it that long?" Selena asked her mom.

"Of course I will. I'd like to see what this trawler yacht can do. Maybe I'll buy one myself."

Selena snuck a glance at Evan, wondering if her mother's cavalier attitude about throwing a large sum of money into a boat on a whim would grate on him. If so, he hid it well.

Evan busied himself prepping the boat to go out on the Gulf. He directed Selena through helping him, while Clara perched on the most comfortable chair on the top deck and watched.

A while later, they were way out in the water, barely

able to see land. Evan had turned the engine off and they drifted. A few other boats were scattered here and there, but they were a good distance from the *Hot Water*. The sun beat down, but the three of them sat on the top deck under a heavy-duty awning. The breeze out here was chilly and Selena was glad she had worn long sleeves.

She leaned her head back on the upholstered seat and breathed in the salty, damp air as the boat rocked freely.

"I'm going to get drinks," Evan said. "I'll be back in a few."

"I'll help you," Selena said.

"No. Sit and relax. It's a one-man job."

Sitting in the fresh air, Selena felt like a bowl of Jell-O, so she didn't argue. Evan disappeared down the narrow stairs and went inside.

"This could be a problem," her mother said.

"What could?" Selena was used to her mother's over-reactions.

"The sway of the boat. I'm feeling a little bit… green."

Selena straightened. "Are you going to throw up?"

"I don't think so. Not now."

"Do you need to lie down or something?"

"I believe I'll go see about some seltzer."

Selena let her follow Evan and closed her eyes again, taking advantage of the solitude, no matter how temporary.

ONCE IN THE PRIVACY of the cabin, Evan let out a long breath, relieved his idea had gone over well with Selena and especially her mom. Nothing would impress the older Jarboe as much as the largest damn boat in the marina, but she seemed okay with the idea of spending the afternoon on the water.

He wondered if he'd jumped to conclusions too soon as the door opened and Mrs. Cambridge-Jarboe entered the living room. She moved slowly and didn't stand quite straight. Must still be getting her sea legs.

"I'd like to talk to you," she said. "In private."

Oh, boy. Here goes something, he thought, though he had no idea what.

"'Course. Have a seat." The galley was open to the living room so he headed in to fix their drinks. He might end up needing a hard one after all. For the moment, he stuck to lemonade.

Instead of sitting in a cozy chair in the living room, Selena's mom climbed on to one of the raised stools at the counter that separated the galley and the living room.

"What are your intentions where my daughter is concerned?"

Evan was filling glasses with ice from the ice maker in the refrigerator and missed. Ice clattered to the wooden floor.

"I told you I've asked her to marry me."

"Yes. Why?"

Evan set the glass down, startled. "Excuse me?"

"Why would you do that? You're young and, from what I can tell, don't know Selena very well at all. I'm going to hazard a guess that it's not because you love her."

"I hate to ruin your rosy view but people do get married for reasons other than love, Mrs. Cambridge-Jarboe."

"I'm all too aware of that. And I'm asking what your reason is."

Evan turned his back to her and pulled the bottled drinks out. As he set them on the counter, he met her eyes. "Selena and I messed up. We're having a baby together. Last I knew, it was considered bad form to desert a woman you got pregnant."

"I'd love some seltzer if you have it. There's a big difference between deserting and committing to spend your whole life with someone."

"Yes. There is. I don't take it lightly, ma'am." He opened the refrigerator again. "Sprite is as close as I've got."

She nodded. "I'm glad to hear you don't take it lightly, but I still want you to make me understand. What are you after?"

Evan set down the bottle he'd been pouring from, fighting to maintain civility. "Why don't you ask me whatever it is you really want to know, Mrs. Cambridge-Jarboe? Enough of this beating around the bush."

The woman stared intently into his eyes and nodded once. "Is it her money?"

Evan dropped his shoulders and chuckled. "Really? You think I'm hanging around for a piece of the bank account she can't access?"

"That's temporary and you know it."

"I know nothing of the sort. I can't begin to understand your relationship with Selena and how money relates to it. I don't want to, frankly."

"But her money would be nice, wouldn't it?"

Evan narrowed his eyes and actually felt his blood pressure rise. "With all due respect, I see a lot of things I like in Selena. Her money isn't one of them. The Selena

I know has two jobs and works her butt off. And that's one of the things I like about her."

She continued to study him. "What else do you like about her?"

Evan had finished pouring the three drinks and stood there, at a loss. He liked plenty, but he didn't figure the things Selena did to him in bed would impress her mother.

Her eyes bored into him and he tapped nervously on the counter.

"I like her guts," he finally said. "I like the way she's determined to make it on her own after leading a somewhat sheltered life. I like when she laughs and I can see there's so much more to her than the beauty on the outside. I like that, despite not being ready for parenthood, she does the best thing for that baby, no matter what."

He picked up two of the glasses. "Excuse me, I'm going to take Selena her drink."

Mrs. Cambridge-Jarboe didn't move, didn't say a word. Until he got to the door to the deck.

"Evan."

He stopped. Turned to look at her, ready to do battle.

She nodded slowly, thoughtfully. "I like you. I hope you can convince her."

Evan nearly stumbled. "Thank you, ma'am." He hesitated, not sure what else to say. "You going to join us?"

"I'm going to sip my drink and hope it settles my stomach. I'll be up in a few minutes."

"Take your time. Being seasick is no fun."

"I'm glad we talked," she said, moving to the couch. "I think we understand each other a little better."

Evan nodded and went outside. Having her mother's blessing was a good thing. Now, if only convincing Selena could be half as easy.

CHAPTER TWENTY

SELENA HAD TO ADMIT she was impressed. Begrudgingly.

Evan had somehow kept her mother happy for the entire afternoon. In spite of her ongoing nausea. Her mom had behaved and had seemed to enjoy being out with them.

Evan had taken the boat north of San Amaro and was heading to the marina in a little burg where a fall festival was going on. The Ferris wheel had caught their attention first, and as they steered in closer, they could see a colorful bouncy castle, a kiddie roller coaster, a merry-go-round and a whole strip of concession stands. The sound of banjo music and laughter reached them as Evan guided the boat into an empty slip.

"Are you going to make it, Mom?"

Clara looked positively pale green. "The driver I called will be in the parking lot. If you get me to the limo, I'll be just fine."

"You've got an hour's drive or so," Evan told her. "Or you could get a room here." By the time she'd surrendered and said she couldn't take any more, this had been the closest place for Evan to dock.

Selena's mother looked around at the town and wrinkled her nose. "I'll be fine. I'll just stretch out in the back and sleep."

Selena nodded. "If she can turn up her nose at the hotel, she's okay."

"Hey," her mom said. "I didn't turn up my nose."

"And the Pope isn't Catholic."

Evan grinned and then called out orders for Selena to help him tie the boat. As soon as they had it secured, her mother was on the dock, muttering her relief. Selena was relieved, too, to be packing her mom off on her merry way. The woman had behaved, relatively speaking, but spending long periods of time trapped on a boat with her was not Selena's idea of a good time. The only bad part of the plan was that once they got Clara on her way, Selena would be left alone with Evan.

Not good.

The limo was easy to find. Not exactly a lot of those in Podunk-ville, Texas. Selena's mom linked elbows with her as they walked.

"Will you call us when you get back? So we know you're okay?" she asked her mom.

"I'm not going to bother you two. I'm already feeling better, just getting off the water. You enjoy yourselves."

Enjoying herself was exactly what Selena was afraid of. She wasn't sure she had the willpower to resist Evan.

"Fine. Call us if you need anything."

They reached the limo and stood a few feet away, waiting for the driver to acknowledge them.

"Evan, thank you for taking us out on the water. I apologize for being a downer."

"You weren't a downer. Next time we'll get you some antimotion sickness pills and one of those metal bracelets that are supposed to help."

Clara looked up at him. "Evan, honey, no offense, but there isn't going to be a next time."

Evan chuckled. "What happened to buying a sailboat?"

"Those plans are off indefinitely."

The driver got out and asked if she was Mrs. Cambridge-Jarboe. As he helped her into the car, she smiled and waved.

"I don't get it," Selena said.

"Get what?" They turned away from the limousine and walked toward the heart of the festival action.

"What you did to her. It's like you two became best friends forever all of a sudden."

"Jealous?"

"Not in the least. You two can have each other. I'll move to Panama."

"You're not running off again," he said.

Selena ignored him.

The sun had dropped below the horizon since they'd docked. The whole park came alive with flashing lights, and live music filled the air. A sinful mix of aromas drifted around them—funnel cakes, cotton candy, hot dogs, tacos. It was warmer on land than it had been out on the water, even though the temperature had dropped with the sun, but Selena pulled her sweater tightly around herself.

"Hungry?" Evan asked.

"Not horribly, after the feast on the boat, but I plan to eat anyway." She grinned, looking forward to some greasy, sugary fair food.

"Which stand do we hit first?" he asked, taking her hand.

He wasn't supposed to hold her hand. She wasn't

supposed to let him. Yet she couldn't bring herself to pull away from his grasp. Holding hands was okay, wasn't it? It was different from kissing. Much different from getting naked. Besides, it was a way to communicate in the noisy crowd. She led him away from the throng of milling people, to the cotton candy stand.

"I should've known you're all about the sugar and fluff," Evan said as they walked up to the counter.

"Not many people get to see my sweet side."

He laughed and she liked the smooth, low sound of it. "Right. Such a mean girl."

"Wait and see. Try to withhold my food from me and you'll suffer the wrath."

"You got me shaking. We're splitting one. This stuff has no substance whatsoever. It can't be good for the baby."

"Better plan to eat your half fast," she taunted.

Evan ordered the cotton candy and they sat on a bench, tearing it apart. By the time they were done, their fingers were sticky and blue. And before she knew what he was doing, Evan took her index finger in his mouth and gently sucked the candy off it.

Selena's body buzzed with awareness. Just from that mouth, that tongue…on her finger? She was so weak.

"That's naughty," she said.

"You want me to stop?" His eyes were alive with mischief and more naughtiness.

She glanced at his lips and then back at those eyes. "Yes. Please."

He nodded. "To quote your mom, when did you turn no fun?"

"I was born no fun."

"I wouldn't buy that if it was on sale. I've seen you doing fun."

Selena couldn't afford to think about the fun he meant. She popped up off the bench and looked down at him. "Are you going to play games with me?"

He looked confused, then got very serious. "I'm not a game player, Selena."

She tried not to smile. "I meant the carnival games. You don't play them? Really?"

"*That's* a different story." He stood. "Which game would you like me to win first?"

"I don't mean to keep harping, but you really need to work on your self-esteem," she said drily. "I think it's holding you back."

He grinned smugly and headed in the direction of Game Lane. Selena followed him, vowing to bring him down.

Two HOURS LATER, they walked slowly toward the marina, Evan carrying an oversize stuffed penguin and holding Selena's hand. She was beyond the point of fighting temptation and had decided she liked touching him, so why shouldn't she? Just for tonight.

"You sure you're okay with that?" Selena asked him, pointing at the penguin and trying to keep a straight face.

"Just fine. Thanks for your concern."

"It's mighty nice of you to haul my winnings, sir."

"Careful. I might accidentally drop Pedro here in the water."

"You know what?" Selena stopped walking and tilted her head. "I'm going to give that bird to you. He's yours. Since you didn't win one and all."

Evan stopped, too, and tried, but failed, to look stern. "You are obnoxious."

"I try." She shivered and ran her hands over her upper arms.

"Getting cold. The boat has a heater."

"Sounds heavenly. Let's hurry."

"Don't rush me. Pedro here is a big burden."

"I know you're not insulting my penguin."

"You said he was *my* penguin."

"If you're going to insult him, you can't have him."

Evan looked down at her in the illumination from the marina lamppost. "Believe me, it's not him I want."

Her body reacted to his words with a longing deep inside. "I think that falls under the 'naughty' category again."

"That keeps happening."

"You should work on it."

They were at the dock where the boat was moored. Evan led her down the narrow walkway, the black water splashing against the supports below. He helped her aboard and steadied her with his hands on her hips as Pedro looked on from the floor of the main deck.

"You said something about a heater?" Selena asked.

"Going be a cold ride home. I have to work at seven tomorrow morning but we just have time to go inside and warm up for a while before heading back."

"I'm not going to argue."

"First time for everything."

"Show respect for the Ring Toss champion, please."

"I ran out of ones. Otherwise I would've dethroned you."

They went through the sliding door into the living

room. Evan turned on a dim lamp on the end table. Selena excused herself to use the restroom.

When she came out of the *head,* as Evan insisted on calling it, into the bedroom, he lay under the blankets on one side of the bed. He flipped the other corner down and patted the mattress. "Electric blanket," he explained.

Selena stared at him, fully clothed, it appeared, stretched out in those satiny black sheets. She got a good eyeful before flipping off the bathroom light switch and sending the room into darkness. The end of the bed was only a couple of feet from the doorway, so she felt her way to him. She sat on the edge of the mattress and kicked her shoes off, then crawled in next to him.

"Feel the heat?" he asked, pulling her close to him.

Lord, did she feel the heat. "Yes. My toes may thaw yet."

She couldn't see him at all yet, as the only light came from a radio alarm clock next to the bed. His breath whispered on her forehead though, and his heart thudded hard in his chest, beneath her hand. They lay, unmoving, in silence, for several minutes. She closed her eyes and focused on the rise and fall of his chest, wondering why he didn't kiss her.

"Selena." His voice was low. Quiet. Strangely comforting. "I owe you an apology."

"You owe the penguin an apology, actually," she said, smiling, not sure she wanted to get into anything serious that might make her think too much. Might talk her out of…this. Being here.

"Pedro will be fine. I'm sorry about the things I said the other day. About your family and your money."

"Okay," she said slowly. "My mom is kind of obnoxious about it, I know. It's hard to ignore."

"A lot of people could let it go, but you deserve to understand where I'm coming from," he said. "I grew up poor, Selena. Dirt-poor would've been a step up."

"I understand—"

"No. You don't. There's no way you could. No offense, but there isn't."

She frowned, acknowledging silently that maybe she didn't. She wanted to, though. "Help me understand, Evan."

He blew out his breath then rolled to his back, putting distance between them. Selena waited.

"My mom didn't have an easy childhood," he began. "She got pregnant young, ended up alone with two all by herself. Life wore her down fast and there was always a question of whether she'd make rent or have enough to feed us. We got evicted several times, ended up sleeping in the car every once in a while—a beat-up station wagon."

Selena listened in horror. She knew people were homeless, knew many didn't get enough to eat. But it'd never been driven home to her so effectively. Even the kids at Art to Heart had homes.

"I'm so, so sorry, Evan. You're right. I can't understand. Can't comprehend how any of you could bear it."

"I'm not proud of it but it's a big part of who I am," Evan said. "I take care of my money. Clay says I hoard it and it's true. I put away every extra cent I can."

Selena found his arm and held on to it as she listened.

"When you said you couldn't pay for good medical

care, it pushed all my buttons. I intended to do whatever I could so you'd have the basics. Whatever you needed."

Selena's heart swelled when she finally realized the extent of how she'd affected him. He'd found out she needed help and he'd been prepared to give it to her no matter what, regardless of the sacrifice. The boat, for one thing.

"Then you found out how well-off my family is," she said regretfully. "And that must've seemed like I was a spoiled drama queen."

"I wouldn't put it that way," Evan said. "It was a shock. What's up with the Saturn? Why not a Bimmer?"

Selena's lips stretched into a half grin. "The Saturn annoyed my mother no end."

"I can imagine. The thing is, finding out about your family made me feel like an idiot. Inadequate."

"You could never be inadequate," she said. If he were inadequate, she wouldn't be in quite the same dilemma now. "At any rate, my mother is hard-core about money, and maybe I came off the same way."

"You're not your mom. You're nothing like her."

"That's the biggest compliment I've ever gotten." The mood lightened as they both laughed.

"She's not *that* bad."

"Yeah, you two were buddy-buddy all afternoon. What did you put in her drink?"

"Not a thing. That was all charm, darlin'."

"You keep talking about that charm, but I'm still waiting to see it."

"I seem to remember charming your panties right off you."

He dipped his hands inside her jeans and below the

panties he was so fixated on. His fingers on her bare skin lit her on fire. She squirmed and arched her body into his.

"Put your money where your mouth is. Or maybe your mouth where your hands are," she said, grinning.

"What kind of guy do you think I am?" His voice had gone husky.

"I'm hoping you're still the naughty kind," she said, barely more than a whisper.

"See now, I've gotten in trouble for being naughty before, so I'm just not sure—"

Selena cut him off with a kiss. Impatiently, she slid her hand up under his shirt, raising it as she ran her fingers from his rock-hard abdomen over the ridges of his chest. She stopped kissing him long enough to whip the shirt over his head, then proceeded to unzip his jeans.

"Oh, no," he said. "You're not the only one who gets to play that game."

Evan lifted her sweater over her head, then unbuttoned and removed her blouse, revealing her lacy dark purple bra. Her eyes had adjusted enough that she could just barely see him. She placed a hand on each side of that beautiful face and admired the angles, the strength of his jaw, the desire that burned in those eyes as they bored into hers. She didn't remember ever taking the time to see him—to really look at him—when they'd made love before. A tangible connection vibrated between them. She felt it in the pit of her stomach, like the instant before you hit a roller-coaster valley, when everything bottoms out and makes you feel as if you're spinning out of control.

The sensation scared her, so she busied herself kissing his lips, nibbling her way to his ear, and then slowly sliding her mouth lower, to his chest. When she circled his nipple with her tongue, he undid her jeans, peeling them down her hips. She helped him get them off her ankles and tossed them to the floor.

Evan rolled her to her back and moved on top of her. He peered into her eyes, his face inches from hers, then smiled as he brushed her hair off her cheek. "Are you sure this is okay? The doctor said so?"

At this point Selena didn't care what the doctor had said, so it was lucky the timing was all right. "It's okay."

He kissed her so gently and thoroughly that her heart went warm and soft. She'd never been kissed like that, full of tenderness and caring, as if he cherished her and wasn't just in this to satisfy his own needs.

"I love looking at you," he whispered, again piercing her with an intense gaze. "I love your eyes, so full of everything you feel at any given moment." He kissed each lid as her eyes fluttered shut, then moved to her mouth.

"I love your lips, especially when you think about kissing me and they part just enough for your breath to rush out in a sexy exhale." He slid his tongue over her lips, inside, keeping his touch light, teasing. Maddening.

He shifted downward, trailing his mouth over her neck and lower. "You're sexy here," he said as he kissed her collarbone.

"My collarbone? Is sexy?" Selena laughed, not sounding anything like her usual soprano self.

"Selena, every part of you is hot. Your little toe turns me on."

His rough hands caressed her sides, then he unfastened the front hook of her bra and pushed it away so her breasts spilled into his hands. "These," he said, alternately running his tongue around the center peak of each nipple, "are perfect in every way. I love watching them pucker when you think dirty thoughts. Love the way they taste like the sweetest aphrodisiac." He took one in his mouth and sucked, making her arch off the mattress.

"I love the way you respond to me."

For her part, Selena loved the way his voice alone could seduce her and his tongue could make her insane with a physical ache. But even more, she loved having him inside her.

"Evan?" Her voice barely worked.

"Yeah?"

"You are making me totally, completely crazy. I love that you love all my bits, but could you maybe… hurry?"

His laugh was low and the sexiest thing she'd ever heard. "Not a chance, darlin'. I want you climbing on the ceiling before I get done with you."

Selena's whimper became a gasp as he returned his attention to her body, continuing his slow descent and telling her every single thing he liked about every single inch of her. When he finally slid her panties off and circled his tongue over the part of her that throbbed for his attention, her every last nerve ending buzzed. It took only moments for her body to shatter around him, and yet she lifted her hips off the bed, begging him to give her more until she couldn't take another second.

She collapsed, and he lay to her side, pulling her into him as she tried to catch her breath. "I don't think

I can move," she whispered, unable to hide a big smile. "You're trying to kill me."

His gravelly voice rumbled in his throat. "Not even close. I'm not nearly done with you."

"Is that a promise or a threat?"

"Yes." He kissed her gently again and she felt his hardness pressing into her thigh. Two minutes ago she'd honestly believed she was spent and wouldn't be able to move again for hours, but just the touch of him had her body responding, tightening…needing him again.

She made short work of getting his pants off him and baring that amazing body. Evan didn't waste any time moving on top of her, kissing her to distraction and pressing his hard body into the softness between her thighs.

"So much for that slow, patient seduction thing, huh?" she teased.

His only response was to enter her. Excellent comeback, she thought, before losing her mind.…

LATER, as they lay with their bodies still connected, hearts pounding, Evan buried his face in Selena's hair, splayed across the pillow. Her scent was intoxicating. Hell, who was he kidding? *She* was intoxicating. Everything about her. Her body, her scent, her words, the sounds she made at the height of passion.

He thought about the conversation he'd had with her mother hours ago and knew he hadn't been completely honest, with himself or with Mrs. C-J.

Reluctantly, he rolled to his side and brought her with him, wrapping his arm around her middle. She settled in with her head against his shoulder. Evan brushed his lips across her forehead and smoothed her hair back.

"I love you," he said. His voice sounded as if it'd been through a rock tumbler. The words were out without any thought, as naturally as if he'd said it before. To anyone. Which he hadn't. He'd never felt like this before, so consumed by another person, hyperaware of her every move when they were together. Absorbed by thoughts of her when they weren't. At first he'd thought it was because, at least partly, she was carrying his child. But now he knew, even if she lost the baby tomorrow, he wanted to be with her.

Selena didn't stir. He had to listen hard to hear her breathing. Maybe she wasn't ready to hear the truth. Her silence told him she didn't return the sentiment—yet.

She would. Soon. He had every confidence in that.

CHAPTER TWENTY-ONE

SELENA WALKED from Evan's truck to the house alone, after asking him not to get out and take her to the door. She'd used the excuses that it was cold and windy and he needed to get home so he could rest before going to work. But they both knew the real reason.

He'd said he loved her.

He couldn't love her. She couldn't afford to love him back.

As she put the key into the lock, the front door suddenly opened, startling the breath out of her.

"Mom," she said. "What are you doing up at—" she checked her watch "—five-fifteen in the morning?"

Her mom went toward the living room, where the lamp and television were both on. "I passed out as soon as I got home. Slept from seven-thirty last night until four and couldn't go back to sleep. Then I realized you weren't home yet."

"I'm home now. Nothing to worry about," Selena said irritably.

"Considering you were out all night with a man who seems to care a lot about you, I'd expect you to be more chipper."

"Yeah, well, the unexpected sucks." Selena made a beeline for her bedroom.

Unfortunately, closing the door didn't keep her pesky mother out.

"We need to talk," her mom said after following her in.

"No, we really don't." Selena wanted to sleep and ignore everything that was swimming around in her head. She crawled in under her blankets, fully dressed, sitting against the headboard.

"What is your problem, Selena? Evan seems like a good man. Handsome, smart, brave. Willing to take care of you and your baby. And yet, you're pulling your usual stunt."

"Oh, I am?" Selena didn't even fake interest, keeping her voice monotone.

"Looks like it to me. You're running away."

"I'm not going anywhere. Yet." She'd definitely considered it, though. The more time she and Evan spent together, the more she thought it would be safer to get away now. Before she cared too much. Before his job caught up with him.

Her mom, wearing mauve silk pajamas, crept onto the other side of her bed and stretched out on top of the covers. "If I thought you didn't care about him, I'd back off. But I think you do. Am I right?"

Selena closed her eyes and wondered when her mom had started giving half a crap about what she did or who she cared for. "I don't suppose you'd just let me go to sleep, would you?"

"Selena! You're going to be a mother in a few months. You need to figure out how you're going to handle that."

"I'm going to have the baby, Mom. Going to do what

everyone else does...try to figure out how to raise a child."

"You could have help."

"Evan?" Selena turned to look at her mom as if she'd grown a horn on the top of her head. "I should marry him so I can have help with the baby?"

"You should marry him because you two make a good couple and I think you're both half in love already."

"It doesn't matter how I feel about him, Mom. Maybe I do love him. I don't know. But it doesn't make a difference."

"Why not?"

"Do you understand what he does for a living?"

"Of course I do. You know very well I married a man with a blue-collar job. One that could kill him."

"And look where that got you." Selena squeezed her eyes shut, willing herself not to think about her dad's death, not to cry. Not now.

"It got me two amazing children. It got me years of happiness and a good marriage with a wonderful man."

"It got you years of loneliness and grief."

Notably, she didn't argue with that. "So you think that, because Evan is a firefighter, he'll die on the job."

"It's a distinct possibility," Selena said, leaning forward. "He goes into burning buildings, Mom. So much could go wrong."

Her mom surprised her by nodding empathetically. "Lots of what-ifs to consider."

"Yes, exactly. And to put a child in that situation, where he or she could lose a father... How can I knowingly do that?"

"You mean like I did," her mother said quietly. "Is that something you've held against me all these years?"

Selena thought about it for a meant. "No, actually. I haven't. The only thing I've held against you is the way you stopped being part of our family as soon as he died."

"We were all affected so much by your dad's death," her mom said, sorrow edging her voice. "You, in particular. You two were so close. You always were a daddy's girl."

"It was devastating," Selena said matter-of-factly. "But just as bad was what happened to you, to us, afterward. What if I'm the same way, Mom? What if I married Evan, something happened to him, and then I shut down, too?"

She dared a glance at her mother in the light of dawn and saw her swallow hard, saw her emotion, her pain. Instead of the usual unemotional mask, the expression remained there, drawing her features downward. Tugging at Selena against her will.

"You won't, Selena." Her voice was lower, quiet, yet firm with conviction.

"How can you know that?" Selena asked.

Her mom sat up in the bed, pulling a throw pillow to her and hugging it. "What I'm about to say I've never told anyone besides my therapist. It's something I don't like to think about and certainly don't like to say out loud."

Selena's internal alarm went off. She and her mom didn't have serious talks.

"Being married to your father, I lived in fear from the time he graduated from the academy. At first I didn't talk about it much. Figured it was my problem. Didn't need to burden him with my fears. Then as time went on, I started to be a little more open."

"I'm sure he knew you were scared for him anyway," Selena said.

"Maybe. But I think they have to approach their jobs very differently. They don't fear them. They can't. They believe they can handle just about anything that's thrown at them. If they went out in the field scared of what might happen, they'd mess up and maybe die."

Selena considered what she said, turned it over in her mind and finally nodded. "Maybe."

"Just before your dad's last assignment, my fear sky-rocketed. One of his colleagues had a close call. I no longer remember the details. I just know it scared the daylights out of me."

Selena thought about the firefighters on the mural. They weren't even colleagues of Evan's, but thinking about the men who had died had heightened her fear for Evan.

"The day before he left, I went a little crazy. I was so afraid for him."

"Did you have a premonition or something?"

Her mother shook her head. "Nothing as concrete as that. Just cold, stark fear. It'd gotten bad enough that I was panicky. And I expressed my fears to your father."

Her mom's voice cracked and tears filled her eyes.

"He tried to comfort me and I wouldn't have any of it. I kept going, building on my fears, making them worse. I started listing all the ways things that could go wrong. Mind you, I didn't know what kind of assignment he was going on, but that didn't matter. My imagination was out of control."

"I can understand that," Selena said honestly.

"The next day he died."

A lump the size of Texas lodged in Selena's throat and she couldn't say a word.

"And I've wondered…" Her mom hesitated, sucking in a shaky breath. "I've thought maybe it was because I opened his mind to doubt. I went through scene after scene of ways someone could hurt him. What if that was enough to put the slightest fear, doubt, into him? What if I was partly to blame for his state of mind and that's what got him killed?"

Tears fell freely down Selena's cheeks and she reached out to hold her mother's hand. "It wasn't your fault, Mom."

"To this day I don't know. God knows I've spent enough on counseling to sort through it but how can I ever believe I was blameless? And the guilt—" Her mom's voice cracked again. "I'm so sorry, Selena. When he died, I could hardly face you and your brother. I felt so responsible. Like every ounce of your pain was my fault. I shut down. It took me years to realize my mistake, to understand what it had done to our family, but by that time, I didn't know how to get you back. How to repair the damage."

For several seconds, maybe minutes, Selena couldn't say anything. Her mother's pain was so evident, something she hadn't seen or understood for all these years. Sure, she knew her dad's death had cut her mom to the quick, just like the rest of them, but…

She couldn't imagine living with the guilt, justified or not.

Selena squeezed her mother's hand. "You weren't responsible for his death, Mom. They're trained to handle the job, regardless of how scared their family may be."

Her mom sniffed indelicately. "Maybe. But that doesn't make me feel any better. It hasn't, all the hundreds of times I've told myself that over the years."

"Forgive me for being dense, but this is supposed to convince me to marry a firefighter...how?" The words came out accompanied by a laugh that sounded more like a sob. "Have you lost your mind?"

"I lost my mind years ago, honey." They both smiled at that. "No. My point, somewhere in that twisted story, is that you can't let your fear rule you. Can't let it get out of control. It's normal to feel scared when someone you love is in a dangerous situation, but you absolutely cannot let the what-ifs run your life. Respect the fear but never let it control you."

Selena stared at her for several seconds. "And how do you do that?"

"I imagine a support network would help. There was a group of FBI wives who got together frequently and I'm sure a big part of it was to connect with others who went through the same emotions."

"I don't remember you going to that."

"I never did. Stupidly, they weren't in my social circle so I didn't think there was any point."

If that wasn't vintage Clara...

"I regret that. Maybe it wouldn't have changed what happened to your father, but then I would've had a support system to help me through it. To help me help you through it." She reached out and ruffled Selena's windblown, bed-messed hair. "That's something I truly regret."

Selena didn't know what to say to that. They'd had

their differences for as long as she could remember and suddenly she was seeing her mom in a different light. One with shadows and nuances she'd never imagined. "I wish you would've talked to me sooner. No matter how hard it would've been. You never gave me the chance to understand."

Her mom did something then that shook her to the core—she broke down into noisy, indelicate sobs, covering her face with her hands but unable to drown out the sounds of sorrow and regret.

"I'm so sorry," her mom said when she could finally manage to speak.

"Shh. You were doing the best you could in really horrible circumstances." Selena found she meant the words. Years of anger melted away as she grasped what her mother had been trying to handle by herself.

Her mom nodded as they wrapped their arms around each other. They stayed like that for several minutes, neither of them speaking. Her mom's crying gradually slowed.

"So. About Evan…that's all you've got for me? Support groups?" Selena wished for a magic answer. A way to make it possible for her to find happiness.

"I've got a little hindsight, as well," Clara said, straightening and smiling sadly. "It helps to understand that this is who these men are. Their careers are as much a part of them as their hair color and their fundamental beliefs."

"Probably true."

"By focusing on the fear, I think we lose sight of that. Become less supportive of them. Maybe even become inclined to try to change them or convince them to do something else."

"You're talking about Tom now, right?" Selena said, missing her brother so much at the mention of him that her chest ached. "I can't count the number of times I've tried to talk him into doing something besides the military."

Her mom nodded. "If he did, it would end up being something just as dangerous, I imagine. Police. Fire department. FBI. You know your brother."

Selena had never been able to think that much about it, but now that she did, she realized her mother was right. "So that's why you never show your fear about his military career."

"Oh, I fear for his life every single day. No mother wants her son to go off to war."

"I couldn't understand why you wanted to throw a party for him."

"Going back into action was important to him. It was either throw a party or go a little more insane from the fear."

Selena nodded slowly. "Why couldn't you tell me this at the time?"

"You weren't exactly listening to me, if you'll recall."

"Maybe." Selena crossed her arms stubbornly. "It doesn't make me feel any better about Tom being over there. Have you heard from him lately?"

"He called a lot at first. Less frequently now. I'm sure he's in the middle of something."

Something. That's what Selena hated. The something could likely get him killed.

"I'm glad we talked," she said. "I think I understand what you're trying to tell me but…" She shook her head. "I don't know. It terrifies me."

"You've got time. The baby isn't due for several months. It won't be easy but you're a strong woman, Selena."

Her mom had never paid her such a compliment and she had to admit she reveled in it. "Thanks, Mom. I don't feel strong."

"I hate to see you let love pass you by, honey. Please tell me you'll try."

Selena thought about the man she did, in fact, love, about how much she wished their future would work out. She nodded. "I will. I'll try."

CHAPTER TWENTY-TWO

THE TENSION in the cab of the truck was thick. Selfishly, Evan hoped it was just the usual uneasiness between Selena and her mother, and not something caused by what he'd said the other night on the boat. He wasn't optimistic, however.

He took the exit to the Harlingen airport and glanced in the rearview mirror at Selena, who rode in the cramped backseat again. She didn't even notice him. Instead she stared out the window with a serious look, as if she was trying to work out how to bring about world peace.

Even though she was in such a serious state, looking at her did things to him. Her gorgeous dark hair fell in waves to her shoulders today. She wore minimal makeup and her lips shone with a clear gloss that smelled of strawberries and vanilla. He longed to see those lips turn up in a smile.

"We're almost there, then?" Mrs. C-J asked, checking her watch for the twentieth time during the hour trip.

"Five more minutes. We'll get you there on time," Evan promised. "Better than your average limo service. Only difference is the size of the backseat."

Her mother laughed but Selena didn't.

Evan parked in the short-term lot and he and Selena

got out to accompany her mother inside—and to help carry the luggage.

"You realize," Evan said as he stacked all the pieces onto a cart inside the door, "that by the time you pay all the extra baggage fees on these, it might be cheaper to buy your own jet?"

He smiled when he said it, still not sure whether Mrs. C-J had a sense of humor. She looked thoughtful and too serious and he wondered if he'd just blown all the goodwill they'd established on the boat.

"You know, you may be right," she said. "All these years, I've been looking for an excuse to buy a private jet but my money manager keeps telling me no. This may just be it. Excellent idea, Evan."

The two of them laughed. Selena forced a smile, shook her head and rolled her eyes. "Don't encourage her spendy side."

They checked her suitcases and walked toward security. Evan did a double take when he noticed Selena's arm interlocked with her mother's. He was glad to see it. She needed her mother more than ever right now and in the not-so-distant future, as she became a mom herself.

At the gate, the two women embraced and held on to each other. He leaned against the wall and gave them all the time they needed.

"Don't forget what we talked about," Mrs. C-J said to Selena.

"I won't." Selena laughed tentatively. "Stuff like that isn't something you just forget about." They pulled apart enough to make eye contact. "Thanks for all that, Mom. I understand better where you're coming from. I'll try to come home for a weekend sometime soon—if you buy the ticket."

Both women laughed. "I'll be happy to." They hugged again and her mother kissed her cheek. "Keep those what-ifs at bay, you hear me?"

"I'll try. I don't know."

"If you ever need to talk, you call me."

Selena looked into her eyes and Evan could tell this was a big moment, suspecting such an offer had never been made before. She finally nodded slowly.

"Love you, Mom."

"I love you, honey."

They parted, and Evan tried not to show surprise when Mrs. C-J turned to him, arms outstretched. He hugged her, her expensive perfume filling his nose. "Take care of my girl, will you?" she said so Selena couldn't hear.

"With pleasure, ma'am."

"What's this 'ma'am' nonsense?" she said, acting scandalized.

They both chuckled.

"I tried to talk some sense into her," she said. "She's stubborn, but I hope she'll come around soon. It would please me no end if the two of you could make it work."

Evan glanced at Selena, who watched them from a few feet away. "Me, too. Have a safe flight, Mrs. C-J."

He moved closer to Selena as they watched her mom go through security. When she'd made it through and put her high-dollar three-inch heels back on, she waved, picked up her carry-on and hurried to her gate. Selena leaned her head on his shoulder and they continued to watch until the older woman was out of sight.

He took her hand and they walked back the way they'd come. "Good visit?" he asked.

Selena didn't answer right away. "I think so. We talked more than we ever have. Resolved some things. She called the bank on the spot yesterday and gave me back access to the family account."

Evan slowed, not really surprised but curious. "So what are you going to do?"

"About?"

"Money. Jobs. Are you going to quit?"

"I have an agreement with the city. Don't worry—I'm not going to flake."

That had crossed his mind, but it wasn't his main concern. "What about the other stuff?"

"SJ Enterprises?"

He nodded, for some reason caring too much about her response.

"I could quit."

"I'm sure your mom will provide you with more than enough money to live on."

"She will. The amount she said she'd transfer to my joint account each month would cover living expenses easily."

Evan thought hard about what life would be like if he and Selena married and she continued to get a check from home each month. Could he live with that? Would he be okay with a wife who didn't believe in working for what she had?

He glanced down at her dark hair and a warmth came over him that he couldn't explain. Not the heat of lust, though that was always there, simmering under the surface. Just looking at Selena brought him a feeling of wholeness he'd never known existed. She made him laugh, made him want to pull his hair out, made him want to be the best person he could be. Made him want to be a father, even. Together, he believed they could raise a happy family, whether Selena had a paying job or not.

She didn't ask for his approval, though, and giving it might seem too much like pressure for her to marry him. He'd promised himself to ease up and give her time, because nothing could convince her to say yes right now. She had to grow to love him and trust him to do everything in his power to come home alive at the end of every shift.

"I'm not going to," Selena said.

"Not going to what?"

"Quit. I love what I'm doing. Love knowing that I can earn my own keep. Once the murals are done, I'll spend less time working. I should be able to handle my business and take care of the baby, too."

If it was possible, he loved her even more at that moment.

"There's no doubt in my mind you'll handle both." Hopefully as his wife.

"I'll set up a special college account for the baby and put the money from my mom in it. If I ever have an emergency, I can dip into my Cambridge-Jarboe funds. But the way Macey and I worked it out, I can make enough to live on within a couple more months."

"Listen to you," Evan said, admiring this new confident professional side.

"What?"

"Ms. Business Chick. Raking in a living."

Selena nodded. "A dose of harsh reality can do that."

They arrived at the exit and went outside to cross the busy taxi and drop-off lanes.

"So what were you and your mom talking about when you said goodbye? Something about what-ifs?"

He unlocked the door of the truck and they both climbed in.

"Somehow you wowed her and I think she wants you for a son-in-law."

He didn't dare hope. "And?"

"She made suggestions for how to deal with a loved one's dangerous career."

He turned and leaned against the driver's door, staring at her. "Loved one?"

She smiled reluctantly. "Yeah. Don't get a big head, though. I could be talking about my brother."

Could be was better than *am*, he supposed.

"What kind of suggestions did she make?"

"Mostly vague ones," she said, her smile fading.

"So do they work?"

She stared straight ahead, biting her lower lip. "I don't know yet. But I'm trying."

That was the best damn news he'd had all day. He nodded, working like the devil to appear nonchalant.

"What do you say we spend the day together while you keep trying?"

"Does your offer include food?"

"As much as you want."

"Ice cream?"

"Butter pecan, all the way."

"You've got yourself a deal, then."

CHAPTER TWENTY-THREE

SELENA HAD spent two days with Evan after seeing her mother off. She'd managed to put all the fears and the what-ifs out of her mind for the most part. She didn't know if it was talking to her mom that enabled it or if she was just in denial. Evan had been off work, so it was easy to pretend they existed in their own little danger-free world.

This morning he'd left her bed to make it to the station by seven. She'd spent the morning painting, trying to catch up from having taken two full days off. After showering, she was warming up a frozen dinner in the microwave.

Her cell phone, plugged in to charge on the kitchen counter, rang out with a bluesy riff that made her heart skip a beat. She hadn't heard the tone for weeks but her body reacted with adrenaline anyway.

"Tom?"

"Yeah, Leenie," her brother said. "It's me."

"Oh my God, what's wrong? Are you okay? You're talking, so you're not dead."

"I'm okay. I've been trying to call you for hours."

Her battery had been dead, and then the phone had been two stories below her. "You must still love me if you're spending all that time trying to get through," she said lightly, over the moon to hear his voice again after so long. Even if she'd been the one to cut him off.

His hesitation registered then and foreboding nearly choked her. "Tom? What's wrong?"

In the two seconds it took him to speak, she thought she would pass out.

"It's Mom. She had an aneurysm last night, Leenie."

She fell onto the sofa, jaw gaping, staring out at the waves but taking no notice of them.

"She died, honey."

"No." She shook her head. "She was just here with me, Tom. She was fine. Perfectly healthy. No way." Her head still shook from side to side, as if she could change the truth if she denied it hard enough.

"Lola found her when she didn't show up for breakfast, but it was too late. She'd apparently passed hours before."

"Oh, God. Poor Lola." Lola was the cook who'd been with them for several years and lived in the guesthouse in the backyard.

"Selena, are you okay?" Tom asked over a static-filled connection.

Was she okay? Her chest tightened until she felt as though a boa constrictor had a hold of her and was seconds from squeezing the life out of her. Tears pricked at her eyes like a thousand tiny pins.

"Mom is…gone?" she said, her voice wavering. "We just… just started getting along better. We talked, Tom. For the first time…"

"I know, Leenie. Look, we have to plan the funeral. I've been on the phone with a funeral home a couple of times but there's only so much I can do from here."

"Where's here?"

"I can't tell you, exactly. But it's remote and hours and hours away from home by plane."

"When will you get home?"

"By the funeral, I hope. I set it for Wednesday. That gives me four days. You need to get a ticket home right away. Do you think you can handle things until I get there?"

She wasn't a helpless spoiled girl anymore. Selena straightened and nodded. "I'll fly out today."

"That's my girl." He had her jot down the name and number of the funeral home. "I'll see you soon, Leenie."

"Bye," she managed, disconnecting the call before dropping her head into her hands.

Unable to face her sadness, she picked the phone up again, saw that it had charged more than halfway, and dialed Evan's cell phone. It went straight to voice mail. Struggling to keep her voice steady, she left a semi-coherent message, telling him about her mother and that she needed to talk to him as soon as possible. Then she grabbed her purse and went out the door, away from the suddenly stifling beach house. Macey worked at the Shell Shack today. She'd make her flight reservations from there, after she calmed down.

"I'LL CLOSE the bar and come with you," Macey said when Selena had finished blubbering all over her shoulder. "I'll get the phone book and we can reserve the flight."

Selena shook her head. "It's okay. I'm going to be okay." She sniffed loudly, not caring that the handful of lunch customers had witnessed her breakdown. Some of them had moved to the patio, either to give her and Macey privacy or to get away from the scene she made. "There's no need for you to go. But thank you so much for offering." She tried to smile, her vision still blurry.

"I mean it, Selena. I can go."

"My brother will be there."

Macey studied her from the stool next to hers. "All right. But if you change your mind..."

"Turn the TV on," a middle-aged guy said as he rushed inside. "There's a big fire on the mainland. Looks like a news helicopter is covering the action."

Macey hopped off the stool, and Selena tried to recover from the terror she'd felt at the word *fire*. If it was on the mainland, though, Evan wouldn't be involved.

"Channel Six," the guy said, as all of them stared at the TV lodged at an angle from the ceiling behind the bar.

When the picture finally appeared, they could see a building engulfed by flames on one side, with so much smoke it was impossible to tell much about where it was.

"It's a school," Macey said. "I've seen that place."

The other customers inside joined them at the main counter from their previous spots around the outer perimeter of the shack.

"Lord have mercy," an older woman said.

"Anyone know what happened?" a man next to her asked.

Macey shook her head and turned the volume up.

"...four-alarm fire here, folks. Departments have been called in from surrounding areas to help. These guys have a long day ahead of them trying to get this fire under control...."

Selena tuned out the rest, stuck on "surrounding areas." She met Macey's eyes over the counter and could see her fear. They were thinking the same thing. Derek was working, too.

The camera panned to what looked like a city park down the block from the burning building. Scads of elementary children were there, along with shell-shocked parents and teachers.

"How'd you hear about it?" another customer asked the man who'd delivered the news.

"Saw it. You can see the smoke from here, and the helicopter."

As the camera panned back to the fire, it passed slowly over the fire trucks, including a big red rig with San Amaro Island Fire Department on the side.

"Oh, God." Selena swallowed down the bile that threatened to choke her. The lights seemed to dim and all sound around her disappeared, as if she'd slipped into a big bubble. Her mouth was completely dry. Her head spun and it suddenly took all her effort to remain upright on the stool.

Macey put her arm around her and pulled her tightly to her side as they were transfixed by the nightmare on the television screen.

"What do we do?" Selena croaked out. "Should we go there?"

Macey shook her head. "We'll get more information here. Trust me, it's chaos there and we don't want to distract anyone."

"We can't just sit here and watch." Without thinking, Selena put her hand over her abdomen.

"They'll be okay," Macey said. Her face was so ashen,

though, Selena knew she was trying to convince herself as much as Selena.

They clung to each other for the next hour. Selena couldn't drag her eyes from the TV.

"Macey." Kevin, one of the shift managers for the bar, hurried in and crossed to her. "I came when I saw the fire on TV. Is Derek on duty?"

She nodded. "Thank you. I could use the help."

The number of customers had doubled, most of them there to get an update on the news.

"Sit down," Kevin said. "Take a break."

"Did you ever eat lunch?" Macey asked Selena as she slid a vacant stool closer.

Selena tried to remember. Then it hit her that her mother had died. God. She'd almost forgotten in the terror of the fire. "No." She felt shaky, as if she could collapse at any second. She held her hand out in front of her and saw it trembling.

Macey sprang into action, but Selena paid no attention. Her vision blurred, and this time it wasn't from tears. There were no tears left inside her—only cold, black fear.

"Come on," Macey said, gently taking her by the arm. "We need to get out of here."

"I need to watch," Selena said, everything swimming in her vision.

"No. Trust me, sweetie. We need some air. I've got you."

Macey pulled her off the stool and firmly propelled her to the doorway on the beach side. Selena didn't even have a chance to look back and check the TV again.

"What if something happens while we're out here?" Selena asked as Macey pulled her closer to the water.

"Then it happens. You looked about to pass out in there. Drink this." She shoved a large plastic cup at Selena.

"I don't want anything."

"It's water. Your body needs it. For the baby if not for yourself."

The baby who could be fatherless. Selena leaned over and threw up into a patch of sea grass.

"Oh, sweetie, come here." Macey led Selena a few steps away and they sat on the chilly sand.

Selena no longer had the strength or the will to stay upright so she lay back on the beach. "How do you do this?" she asked Macey hoarsely.

"I tell myself everything will be okay. Over and over again."

"Do you ever believe it?"

Macey was quiet for a few seconds. "Yes. I think I do. I know Derek is good at what he does. Evan is, too."

"Accidents can happen to good firefighters."

"Sure. But you have to believe they'll do everything they can to handle them."

Selena didn't respond. She bent her knees toward the sky and closed her eyes, her hands burrowing through the sand. Her chest ached and her neck and the base of her skull felt as though someone had repeatedly taken an ax to them.

Macey looked down at her and rubbed her hand over Selena's sandy one. "Try taking twenty deep breaths. It helps with the panic."

Selena was on inhale number four when they heard a gigantic boom in the distance. It was like a cannon but twenty times louder. She shot upright and

Macey whipped around, trying to figure out what had happened.

Macey swore, something Selena had never heard her do, as she hurried to her feet and held out a hand for Selena.

"What? What was that?"

"Maybe an explosion. Come on."

"Oh, God." Where she found the energy to run back to the bar, she didn't know, but they got there in time to hear the news announcer on the TV say that an explosion had rocked the school building.

"The last we knew, there were rescue personnel inside the building still attempting to get people out. We'll keep you posted as we get answers. A lot of questions and unknowns here, folks."

Kevin came up to them and put his hands on Selena's and Macey's. "You girls holding up?"

Selena couldn't answer aloud but no, she wasn't holding up at all, thank you very much. If something happened to Evan...

"Could you get her something to drink?" Macey asked. "Nonalcoholic, please. She's pregnant."

If Kevin was surprised, he didn't show it. He filled a cup with Sprite, stuck a lid on it and slid it in front of Selena.

"Drink," Macey said.

"We have confirmation that two rescue personnel are being taken to the emergency room with injuries," the man on the TV said. "We don't have word on the extent of the injuries yet. Stay tuned."

"Let's go," Macey said, grabbing the Sprite with one hand and Selena with the other. "Kevin, could you hand me my purse? It's in the drawer in back."

They made their way to the door closest to the parking lot. Kevin met them there with the bag. "Call me, Mace."

She nodded and they hurried to her car.

IT TOOK more than two hours for them to find out that the men brought in were firefighters but not *their* firefighters. One was in critical condition and the other was expected to make it but had severe burns. They were both from the department on the mainland, not San Amaro. Selena and Macey didn't know the men or their families, but that didn't diminish the bone-deep sorrow Selena felt for those involved. Still, she was relieved, at least for now, that Evan and Derek weren't the men in the E.R. with a whole team of doctors working on them.

A wave of exhaustion nearly brought Selena to her knees as they walked out to Macey's Corolla. "I think I need to go home."

"You look like you got dragged by a train."

"That's actually better than I feel."

"Want me to stay with you?"

Selena fell into the passenger seat and considered it. "I love you for offering, but I just need to go to bed."

"I'll call you when I hear something."

"Please." Though if it was any more bad news, Selena didn't have a clue how she would survive it.

CHAPTER TWENTY-FOUR

IT WAS PITCH-DARK when Selena's cell phone jolted her awake.

She felt around for it on the nightstand, disoriented and scared to death of whoever was calling.

Don't let it be bad news.

Her heart was going Indy 500 speeds and her ears buzzed in between rings. It was as if she was trapped at the bottom of a well and the oxygen supply was almost gone.

"Yeah?" She sat up on the edge of her bed, her feet hitting the floor.

"Selena, it's Macey. They've got the fire under control. Still some hot spots but our guys are back at the station."

"Evan?"

"He's okay. Derek, too." Her voice was full of pent-up emotion. "They're okay, sweetie."

"Thank God." Selena turned on the lamp. "Where are you?"

"I'm at the station. Derek's in the shower right now. I'm waiting to see him."

"Have you slept yet?" Selena asked.

"No. But I'm going to sleep like a baby now, I promise you." Macey sniffed. "Evan rescued a little girl, Selena. He saved her life."

Selena smiled through the tears that coursed down her face as she slid to the floor. "That's so great." She closed her eyes. "What a man he is. They all are."

"Got that right."

"Go get Derek. And thanks for calling me."

Selena ended the call and sat there, dazed, for several minutes. The alarm clock told her it was 2:14 a.m. She'd crashed hard in her bed, comalike, sleeping for several hours.

Slowly, she rose and changed clothes, since she hadn't had the energy to get her pajamas on before. As she dressed, she made a decision.

Selena pulled out one of her carry-on bags and stuffed in a change of clothes and her toiletries, having finally booked a flight last night for seven this morning. She'd left enough of her cold-weather clothes back in Boston to get by. She ran a brush through her hair and clipped it back, then shoved her feet into shoes. On her way out the door, she grabbed her coat and purse and slung the tote over her shoulder.

The half-mile drive to the station seemed longer than it had in the past. Surreal. The rest of the world slept while her heart thundered. She had to see Evan. Had to assure herself he was unharmed. Had to tell him what had become crystal clear to her upon waking.

EVAN STOOD alone in the shower, scrubbing his body yet again in an attempt to get rid of the soot that seemed to cover every inch of him. His lungs screamed from too much smoke, but the damage was negligible. Especially compared to the others.

Two men had gone down tonight, one of them still

fighting for his life. They'd also pulled out two civilian victims. A teacher who'd helped her students escape and a first-grade girl who'd hidden in one of the restrooms when the fire broke out. He'd seen one of the bodies being carried slowly to the ambulance as he'd gotten new orders. He'd seen dead victims before, but it would always tear him apart to know there was someone they hadn't been able to save.

Thank God he'd found the other little girl when he had. He'd been able to get her out and to the paramedics in time. Last he'd heard, when they returned to the station, she was doing okay at the hospital. It was his first rescue—he'd waited years for the timing and the circumstances to line up in his favor. Satisfaction and gratitude had overwhelmed him after he'd gotten her out, but word of the victims and the injured firefighters had dampened his elation soon after.

He poured more shampoo into his hand and massaged it into his hair. The stench of smoke was impossible to get rid of entirely and it made his nostrils burn. After another round of soap, he finally turned the water off. His skin was as clean as he could get it tonight.

As the shower spit out a few last drops of water, Evan stood there, one hand still on the knob, leaning his forehead and forearm against the wall. He was spent now that the adrenaline had stopped pumping.

He heard something behind him and turned around.

Selena stood there, hair a mess, eyes shining with tears.

"What are you doing here, darlin'?"

"They said you were alone. That I could come in." Her voice was quiet, unsure. Tired.

"It's fine," he said, walking toward her, still dripping wet. He'd never been so damn happy to see her, in spite of her drawn face and haunted eyes.

She hesitated for a moment, then closed the gap between them and wrapped her arms around his naked body, buried her head against his wet chest. And began sobbing.

"Selena, it's okay. I'm fine. Everything's going to be fine." His voice was gravelly as hell from all the smoke.

She just held on and cried. By the time she'd quieted down, he was mostly dry except for the part of his chest she'd drenched with tears.

Selena looked down at her damp clothes and then met his eyes. Hers were red rimmed and bloodshot. Evan brushed her hair behind her ear and held her hand as he walked over to the stack of clean towels. He wrapped one around his waist then pulled her to him again. She began to cry, even harder.

"Selena, what's wrong? The fire's over. We saved some people—a girl and a boy."

She nodded up against him. "S-sorry. Did you get my message?"

"What message, darlin'?"

"On your phone."

He wasn't even sure where his phone was. "Not yet."

She inhaled slowly, shakily, and those brown eyes lined with damp lashes sought his again. "My mom d-died. Last night. Aneurysm."

Oh, holy hell. He took both her hands and pulled her

out of the shower area to a dry bench. He straddled it next to her and hugged her again. "I'm so damn sorry, Selena."

She cried silently, shoulders jerking up and down, for another few minutes. Gradually the tears began to subside, but he didn't let go. He didn't have the first notion of what to say.

"Sorry about that," she said finally, sounding much stronger than before. "I didn't mean to cry."

"Shh. It's okay."

She stood and took two steps away from him. "It's not okay, actually. I...Evan...I can't do this anymore. I'm not cut out to be a firefighter's wife."

He felt her words like a dull knife to the gut. "Everything worked out, Selena. I'm fine. Look at me."

"Two of your colleagues aren't, Evan. What if that had been you?"

"It wasn't. This was a particularly bad fire, darlin'. Every time won't be like this."

She shook her head. "There won't be an every time. I can't do it." She stood taller. "I won't, Evan. Today was torture. I know it wasn't a cakewalk for you, but you've chosen this life. I haven't."

"You won't even give it some time before you decide?"

"There's no point. I can't live like this. I'm flying home for the funeral and when I get back, there won't be an us."

"So you *are* coming back to San Amaro?"

"I have commitments here. The murals. My business."

"I'm not giving up," Evan said, his throat raw with pain, both physical and other.

Selena stared at him, then slowly, sadly shook her head. "I have to go now. Goodbye, Evan."

He watched her walk, step by graceful step, out of his life.

CHAPTER TWENTY-FIVE

"You doing okay?"

Selena looked up at her brother from where she sat on the main stairway in the Cambridge-Jarboe family estate. She nodded distractedly. "I guess. All things considered."

"All things considered," Tom repeated, gesturing for her to move over so he could sit next to her. "Lots to digest."

"You're still freaking out because I'm pregnant, aren't you?"

"Hell, yeah. You're my baby sister. I'm going to be an uncle."

They'd stayed up talking most of the night before after getting through the funeral, the burial, the gathering at the house afterward. The ordeal had made time disappear and brought their father's death back as if it'd happened the week before instead of fifteen years ago.

"You'll be the best uncle ever," she said, leaning into him. "You can buy him baby camos."

Tom chuckled. "The question is whether you'd let the little one wear them or not."

"As long as you don't start recruiting before high school."

"I wouldn't dare. Don't need that big bad firefighter coming after me."

Selena grinned reluctantly. "You big bad Army guys have a problem with big bad firefighters beating you up?"

"Actually, not in this lifetime. I'm more afraid of the firefighter's woman."

"I'm not his anything, Tom. I told you that."

"What would he say about that?"

"I don't want to talk about it anymore. When do you go back?"

"Day after tomorrow. Sorry I can't stay longer, but I was lucky to make it back at all."

"I know. Thank God you did. I couldn't have gotten through it without you."

"You're a lot stronger than you give yourself credit for."

His words reminded her of what her mother had said and choked her up. She changed the subject. "There's a lot of work to be done here if we're really going to sell this place."

"You still want to, after sleeping on it for two whole hours?"

Selena nodded. "You?"

"I don't need a place like this. Compared to what I'm used to, the guesthouse is like a luxurious resort."

"This place has always been Mom's. She loved it. The rest of us just…lived here."

"I want you to forget about sorting through anything right now," Tom said. "We can do it later, when my deployment's over, after your baby is born."

"What if you don't—" Selena stopped herself.

"What?" Tom asked.

Selena looked around, a sad grin on her face, half expecting to see her mother. "You'll make it back just fine. Right?"

"Hell, yeah. Nothing's going to stop me from meeting my nephew."

"Or niece."

"You keep calling it him."

Just like Evan did. If this little one was a girl, she'd have an adjustment to make.

She studied her brother, thinking about the conversation she and her mother had had just about a week ago. "Of all the people in our family, Mom had the safest existence. The most dangerous thing she did was fly cross-country to track me down."

"Yeah. You take after her, Leenie. You are one risk-averse chick."

"And yet, she's the one who died. Of a freaking random blood clot." Her voice thickened in her throat and it was all she could do to get the words out.

"Can happen to any of us," her brother said, putting his arm around her.

"I was so busy worrying about you and Evan, I didn't even think about something happening to Mom."

"Wait a sec," Tom said, removing his arm and leaning away to frown at her. "You mean even though you took off to Texas to get me and Mom out of your life, you've still been worrying about me?"

Selena didn't meet his eyes. "Every stinking day."

Tom clunked his head back against the wall. "Then why in the hell did you feel it was necessary to cut me off? If you were worrying anyway..."

For the two-thousandth time that week, tears blinded Selena.

"All I wanted was to hear your voice sometimes. Make sure you were doing okay," her brother continued. "I thought you walked away so you wouldn't have to worry."

Selena laughed...or was she crying? She wasn't sure, but her shoulders shook. "I know. I thought I could handle things better by disappearing."

"But no?"

"But no."

Definitely crying. Out-of-control crying.

Tom held on to her forearm and let her get it out as she sat there sobbing hysterically for a good five minutes. When she calmed down, hiccuping on a half sob only periodically, he started in.

"So. Let's review. You worried about me."

"Yes."

"You cut me off so you wouldn't have to worry about me."

"Yes." Selena grinned at his theatrics in spite of herself.

"And yet you kept right on worrying about me, even though you ran thousands of miles away."

"Yes."

He looked at her, nodding, as if to say he was onto her game now. "And this firefighter dude..."

Oh, no, not this.

"Evan? You worry about him?"

She nodded halfheartedly, knowing exactly where her pain-in-the-butt brother was going with this.

"Sooo, the brainiac who is my sister has once again

decided that if she cuts him out of her life, she will worry less. Correct?"

She didn't answer. Because she knew he was absolutely right. And while the thought scared the ever-loving daylights out of her, it also sparked intense hope.

Tom raised one eyebrow at her, something he'd always done because he knew it drove her crazy.

"Don't give me the brow," she said.

He didn't stop.

"You think I'm being foolish."

"Absolutely ridiculous. Outrageous." He smiled and then grew serious. "Selena, caring for someone is never easy. But if you focus on the positive instead of dwelling on the negative—"

"The what-ifs," she said, nodding. "Mom said the same thing."

"You know what, Leenie? For once, Mom was right."

The fear was still there in her gut, but it was being drowned out by possibilities. She bolted off the stairs and paced at the foot of them. Nodding to herself. "I can do this. I can stop with the what-ifs and all the other bad thoughts. Macey can help me—she seems good at it. She could be my support group, just like Mom said…"

"Selena?" Tom was still perched on the step, watching her in obvious amusement.

She stopped pacing. "What?"

"You can do it. And if, God forbid, something bad ever happens to someone you love—like Mom, Dad— you can get through it. It sucks royally, but you can get through it. You're one of the strongest women I know."

"I'm not."

He stood and towered over her. "Don't argue with me." The smile on his face contradicted the bellow of his voice.

"I love him, Tom."

"Then go tell him that." He came down the bottom three steps and hugged Selena. "Get out of here."

She looked up at him, smiling so wide it hurt. "I think I will."

"Will you marry me?"

Smiling, Evan peered down at the half-pint girl. "I'll tell you what, Angelica. When you get old enough to get married, you come find me. If I'm still single, we can talk, okay?"

The brown-haired girl with beautiful eyes nodded enthusiastically. "'Kay. Can I drive the truck now?"

"Angelica, Señor Drake has shown us everything and given us the very best tour," her mother said. "It's time for us to go."

"You know what, Angelica? I don't even get to drive the truck most days."

"Really?" She frowned and looked around, as if she was going to set things right for him.

"I have other jobs. Like rescuing very important little girls like you."

She nodded emphatically at his excellent point. He glanced at her mother again, laughing to himself until he saw Mrs. Hernandez was almost in tears.

"We are so very grateful for what you did," she said, her English heavily accented.

"I'm just glad we got her out quickly. She's doing so well."

"Thanks to you. Can I hug you, please?"

"Me, too!" Angelica skipped over from the truck.

Evan hugged the woman briefly, then bent down to the little girl. She wrapped her arms around his neck and didn't seem to plan to let go anytime soon. As he crouched there with her, someone outside the garage caught his attention.

His heart reacted almost before he realized who it was. What was Selena doing here?

"You take care of your mommy, you hear me?" he said to Angelica, easing her away.

"Yes, sir!" she yelled. It was hard to believe this was the girl who'd been drifting in and out of consciousness when he pulled her from the burning school just a week ago.

"Thanks for coming by so I could see you again. Drop by anytime, okay?"

"Yes, sir!"

Both he and Mrs. Hernandez laughed. They said goodbye and the woman and her daughter went toward the parking lot, leaving Evan by himself, staring at the woman he loved.

He braced himself for whatever it was she was here to say to him and headed outside.

"Hey, hero," she said, standing there looking breathtakingly gorgeous. She wore a long, loose dress the bluish-green color of the Gulf and, when he looked closely, he could tell for the first time she was carrying a baby. *His* baby. Just like that something major shifted inside him at the thought of meeting his child.

"Welcome back. How did everything go?"

"As well as a funeral can go. Do you work until to-morrow morning?"

"Actually, I'm not on duty. That little girl, Angelica, is the one we pulled out from the school. Her mama brought her in for a tour and she insisted on me giving it to her, so the guys called and asked me to come up for it."

She grinned, squinting in the bright sun. "She's got herself a case of hero worship."

"Asked me to marry her, as a matter of fact."

Her smile turned into a frown and she swore mildly.

"What's wrong, Selena?" He moved closer, thinking maybe she'd had some pain, maybe something was wrong with the baby.

"It's just that…I was hoping it would be me."

"What would be you?"

"The one who married you."

He stared at her, his mouth probably gaping open like an idiot, as her words sank in.

"Say that again, please."

"I know you're a big local hero and all, with groupies and fan girls—of all ages, apparently—but I was kind of thinking that since you asked me to marry you first, before her…"

Evan grinned. Laughed. Threw his head back and howled. "Lucky for you, I didn't accept her proposal outright. I'm still available."

"Excellent. Because this baby and I, we need a third. A man of the house. Someone to kill spiders and change lightbulbs."

He stepped closer and put his arms around her, squeezing her and lifting her off the ground. He spun her around in a circle, then checked the windows, praying to God that none of the guys were gawking at them.

Sure enough, Rafe and Luis stood in the kitchen avidly watching him and Selena.

Ah, to hell with it. He grinned, waved at the guys, then picked up Selena and spun her again. As he slid her back to her feet, he kissed that beautiful head of hair, breathing in her intoxicating peaches-and-vanilla scent. He took her hand and led her away.

"Where are we going?" she asked.

"Away from our audience. Like a bunch of damn gossip girls standing there staring."

Selena glanced over around him, laughed and waved at the others.

They walked around the wall to the side with the finished mural and sat on the pavement, out of sight from the gawkers.

"This isn't close enough," Evan said. "I've had to live without you for a week. I want you here." He pulled her up onto his lap.

"Better?" she asked, her slightly swollen belly the only thing between them now.

"Much. So tell me. What changed your mind? Nothing's different about my career. I still have to fight the occasional big, bad fire."

She nodded. "I know."

"And you're okay with that? You think you can handle it?"

"I'm okay with it. It's who you are, Evan. What you

do. If you did anything different, you wouldn't be the man I fell in love with."

He stared into her eyes, feeling himself falling deeper and not caring. "All true," he said huskily.

"I tried running away from my brother, to avoid the fear that something terrible would happen again, but it didn't work. I still worried every day. And I missed him."

"I'd like to meet him."

"Oh, you will. You two are exactly alike. All about danger and heroism. Blah, blah, blah."

"He sounds like one cool dude."

"You would say that." She wove the fingers of their hands together, becoming serious again. "I never expected my mom to die such an untimely death." She sucked in a quick breath and he guessed she was struggling not to cry. He tightened his grip on her hands. "I'm so glad she and I had those last few days together, Evan. It's like we made our peace." She sniffed and met his gaze directly. "It made me realize we never know how long we'll have people in our lives. So however long you have, I want you to be mine."

"I'm yours, darlin'." Evan pulled her in for a lingering kiss.

Selena backed away after several seconds. "Just get this through your head. You better be careful, and you better come home to me after every single shift. If you get yourself hurt, I will kick your ass."

Evan laughed. "You better hope I'm not the kind of guy who likes it rough."

"Cute," she said sarcastically. "I mean it. This baby needs his father. And so do I."

"You need me?" Evan said with a wide grin.

"I need you. More than I need anyone or anything else in the world."

"More than ice cream?"

Selena paused. Tilted her head and put her finger to her lower lip thoughtfully. Nodded. "Yes, although ice cream's a close second."

Evan wrapped his arms around her as if he would never let her go. "How 'bout we go celebrate with some butter pecan?"

"You do so know the way to this woman's heart."

EPILOGUE

"WHAT'S WITH the Mystery Woman thing, darlin'? Where are we going?" Evan asked.

Selena got out of the truck, unfastened the car seat belt and pulled three-month-old Christian—named for her father—into her arms. She handed the baby a key ring to jingle and chew on. "Thirty's a milestone birthday. We have to celebrate appropriately."

Evan looked at her sideways, as if he wasn't sure whether to trust her, and Selena taunted him with a sneaky laugh.

"This way," she said.

"Want the stroller?" Evan asked. "Champion Eater is a load these days."

She shook her head. "We don't need that where we're going."

"Which is...where, exactly?"

"I never knew you were so impatient. It's cute."

"I've got your cute right here, darlin'. Which way?"

Instead of answering, Selena walked toward the marina, the same route they'd taken almost a year ago when they had gone on their adventure with her mom.

"Aha," Evan said as they rounded the corner of the building and the boats came into sight. "I've got it. We're taking Chief's boat out for a birthday spin. You going to drive?"

Selena kept walking. When she passed the second dock where the fire chief moored his boat, she surreptitiously watched her husband. His brow furrowed. He searched the boats at dock number two and did indeed locate the *Hot Water*. Then he narrowed his eyes. She put on her most innocent act and continued in silence.

At dock four, she angled out over the water, slowing so that Evan caught up to her. Christian stared at his daddy with big blue eyes and chubby cheeks.

"Hey, little man. I suppose you know the secret, too, huh? Anything you want to tell Daddy?"

"Gah!"

"See anything you like?" Selena asked, gesturing to the boats with her head.

Evan turned his attention from his son to the scenery and immediately homed in on the Grand Banks trawler yacht at the end of the line. *The Fire and Ice Cream*.

"That one's new here. Never seen it before. I would remember that." He whistled. "She's a beauty."

"Give that to Daddy," Selena coaxed Christian. "Go ahead, sweetie. Give Daddy the keys."

Evan reached for the ring that Christian and Selena held out together. He still had the over-the-moon new-dad look about him, the one he'd worn the entire past three months. "Thank you," he said, distracted.

Selena could see the instant when the realization dawned on him. His expression changed from baby love to *whoa*.

"Selena?" Evan said. "Want to tell me what's going on?"

She laughed and walked onto the narrow dock to the back end of the *Fire and Ice Cream*. At her nod, the door to the cabin flew open and Melanie, Brad and Henry, and Evan's mother, Susan, burst out onto the deck.

"Surprise!"

"Hell," Evan said shakily. "Oh, God. Selena?"

"It's yours, Evan. I thought we'd let you take your new boat for a spin. Your mother needs a ride home to Tampa."

The look on his face was second only to the expression he'd had at the moment Christian had been born. Like a little kid, Evan hopped over to the deck and spun around, laughing. He climbed up to the captain's chair and ran his hands over the dashboard and controls. Then he climbed back down and disappeared into the cabin, while Selena and the rest of his family stood outside high-fiving and laughing for all they were worth.

"You got him good, Selena," Melanie said. "I love it!"

Selena took Christian inside. Evan was already down a level, checking out the staterooms and howling his approval every few seconds. She went down to revel in his excitement.

"You like it?" she asked.

"Do I like it?" He threw his arms around her and the baby and spun around awkwardly in the small space. "You're never going to get me off this thing! Is it really ours?"

"One hundred percent. Made possible by the sale of my mother's house. She never got to buy her own boat or plane, but I know she'd love nothing more than to spoil you like this."

"It's perfect."

"I know it's been your dream for a long time."

"Darlin', you've already made my dreams come true.

Twice before today." He took Christian from her and raised the baby above his head, then lowered him into a hug. "Thank you. It's going to take me the next hundred years to repay the favor."

Selena shook her head. "Nope. You already have."

He pulled her close with his available arm and kissed her long and slow.

She smiled against his lips and said, "We're even."

* * * * *

Want to read more from Amy Knupp
about The Texas Firefighters?
Don't miss Clay Marlow's story,
FULLY INVOLVED, in September 2010!
Available wherever Harlequin books are sold.

HARLEQUIN *Super Romance*

COMING NEXT MONTH

Available September 14, 2010

#1656 THE FIRST WIFE
The Chapman Files
Tara Taylor Quinn

#1657 TYLER O'NEILL'S REDEMPTION
The Notorious O'Neills
Molly O'Keefe

#1658 FULLY INVOLVED
The Texas Firefighters
Amy Knupp

#1659 THIS TIME FOR KEEPS
Suddenly a Parent
Jenna Mills

#1660 THAT LAST NIGHT IN TEXAS
A Little Secret
Ann Evans

#1661 ONCE A RANGER
Carrie Weaver

HSRCNM0810

LARGER-PRINT BOOKS!
GET 2 FREE LARGER-PRINT NOVELS PLUS
2 FREE GIFTS!

HARLEQUIN®

Super Romance®

Exciting, emotional, unexpected!

YES! Please send me 2 FREE LARGER-PRINT Harlequin® Superromance® novels and my 2 FREE gifts (gifts are worth about $10). After receiving them, if I don't wish to receive any more books, I can return the shipping statement marked "cancel." If I don't cancel, I will receive 6 brand-new novels every month and be billed just $5.44 per book in the U.S. or $5.99 per book in Canada. That's a saving of at least 13% off the cover price! It's quite a bargain! Shipping and handling is just 50¢ per book.* I understand that accepting the 2 free books and gifts places me under no obligation to buy anything. I can always return a shipment and cancel at any time. Even if I never buy another book from Harlequin, the two free books and gifts are mine to keep forever.

139/339 HDN E5PS

Name _____ (PLEASE PRINT) _____

Address _____ Apt. # _____

City _____ State/Prov. _____ Zip/Postal Code _____

Signature (if under 18, a parent or guardian must sign) _____

Mail to the Harlequin Reader Service:
IN U.S.A.: P.O. Box 1867, Buffalo, NY 14240-1867
IN CANADA: P.O. Box 609, Fort Erie, Ontario L2A 5X3

Not valid for current subscribers to Harlequin Superromance Larger-Print books.

Are you a current subscriber to Harlequin Superromance books
and want to receive the larger-print edition?
Call 1-800-873-8635 today!

* Terms and prices subject to change without notice. Prices do not include applicable taxes. N.Y. residents add applicable sales tax. Canadian residents will be charged applicable provincial taxes and GST. Offer not valid in Quebec. This offer is limited to one order per household. All orders subject to approval. Credit or debit balances in a customer's account(s) may be offset by any other outstanding balance owed by or to the customer. Please allow 4 to 6 weeks for delivery. Offer available while quantities last.

Your Privacy: Harlequin Books is committed to protecting your privacy. Our Privacy Policy is available online at www.eHarlequin.com or upon request from the Reader Service. From time to time we make our lists of customers available to reputable third parties who may have a product or service of interest to you. If you would prefer we not share your name and address, please check here. ☐

Help us get it right—We strive for accurate, respectful and relevant communications. To clarify or modify your communication preferences, visit us at www.ReaderService.com/consumerchoice.

HSRLP10R

HARLEQUIN®

A *Romance*

FOR EVERY MOOD™

Spotlight on
── Heart & Home ──

Heartwarming romances
where love can happen
right when you least expect it.

See the next page to enjoy a sneak peek
from Harlequin Superromance®,
a Heart and Home series.

Enjoy a sneak peek at fan favorite Molly O'Keefe's
Harlequin Superromance miniseries,
THE NOTORIOUS O'NEILLS, *with*
TYLER O'NEILL'S REDEMPTION,
available September 2010
only from Harlequin Superromance.

Police chief Juliette Tremblant recognized the shape of the man strolling down the street—in as calm and leisurely fashion as if it were the middle of the day rather than midnight. She slowed her car, convinced her eyes were playing tricks on her. It had been a long time since Tyler O'Neill had been seen in this town.

As she pulled to a stop at the curb, he turned toward her, and her heart about stopped.

"What the hell are you doing here, Tyler?"

"Well, if it isn't Juliette Tremblant." He made his way over to her, then leaned down so he could look her in the eye. He was close enough to touch.

Juliette was not, repeat, *not* going to touch Tyler O'Neill. Not with her fingers. Not with a ten-foot pole. There would be no touching. Which was too bad, since it was the only way she was ever going to convince herself the man standing in front of her—as rumpled and heart-stoppingly handsome now as he'd been at sixteen—was real.

And not a figment of all her furious revenge dreams.

"What are you doing back in Bonne Terre?" she asked.

"The manor is sitting empty," Tyler said and shrugged, as though his arriving out of the blue after ten years was casual. "Seems like someone should be watching over the family home."

"You?" She laughed at the very notion of him being here for any unselfish reason. "Please."

He stared at her for a second, then smiled. Her heart fluttered against her chest—a small mechanical bird powered by that smile.

"You're right." But that cryptic comment was all he offered.

Juliette bit her lip against the other questions.

Why did you go?

Why didn't you write? Call?

What did I do?

But what would be the point? Ten years of silence were all the answer she really needed.

She had sworn off feeling anything for this man long ago. Yet one look at him and all the old hurt and rage resurfaced as though they'd been waiting for the chance. That made her mad.

She put the car in gear, determined not to waste another minute thinking about Tyler O'Neill. "Have a good night, Tyler," she said, liking all the cool "go screw yourself" she managed to fit into those words.

It seems Juliette has an old score to settle with Tyler.
Pick up TYLER O'NEILL'S REDEMPTION
to see how he makes it up to her.
Available September 2010,
only from Harlequin Superromance.

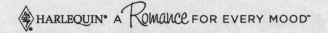

HARLEQUIN®
Super Romance®

Watch out
for a whole new look for
Harlequin Superromance,
coming soon!

*The same great stories you love
with a brand-new look!*

Unexpected, exciting
and emotional stories
about life and falling in love.

Coming soon!